CW01510601

FALLEN
FEATHERS

—

Adam Howorth

Troubador Publishing Ltd
Unit E2 Airfield Business Park,
Harrison Road, Market Harborough,
Leicestershire. LE16 7UL
Tel: 0116 2792299
Email: books@troubador.co.uk
Web: www.troubador.co.uk

ISBN 978 1836280 088

British Library Cataloguing in Publication Data.
A catalogue record for this book is available from the British Library.

Printed and bound by CPI Group (UK) Ltd, Croydon, CR0 4YY
Typeset in 11pt Adobe Garamond Pro by Troubador Publishing Ltd, Leicester, UK

For Grace Elizabeth

Love children especially, for they too are sinless like the angels; they live to soften and purify our hearts and, as it were, to guide us.
(Fyodor Dostoevsky, *The Brothers Karamazov*)

ONE

Under a Corn Moon

When he was a boy, Edward wanted to be a farmer like his father. That was, until one summer when he was in the fields behind his home and saw a man coming up the track. He was riding a brown-and-white horse that walked slowly, catching the dirt with its hooves, and Edward had the strange feeling that this moment had come before.

'Hello, young man,' the man said, pulling on the reins. 'Enjoying this fine weather, I see.'

'I'm checking the corn for my father,' Edward replied. 'There should be at least twenty grains on every head.'

The man laughed. 'Very good; so there should.'

They looked at each other and Edward felt he should say something else.

'You have sad eyes.'

The horse lifted its head and bared its teeth. It sighed heavily, expelling the air through flared nostrils. Edward watched the fine mist from the animal's lungs dissolve in the sunlight. He knew better than to make personal comments but was unable to help himself.

'That's all right, girl,' the man said, patting the horse on the neck. 'There is truth in what you say, child.' He turned to Edward and smiled, but the boy saw no happiness. 'My eyes see the sins of the world and that makes me sad. But like you, they also find beauty in a blade of corn. Turn it slowly in your hands and watch the light dance on the grains.'

Edward did as he was told and saw the contours of each kernel come into focus as it caught the sun.

'Where you find beauty, there is hope. It doesn't matter how many times we cut the corn and burn the straw; when the sun returns and the rains touch the soil, the fields of gold will return.' The man pulled again on the reins, pointing the horse back up the track.

'Where are you going?' the boy asked.

'Wherever I am needed,' the man replied, attempting a smile again.

A pair of swallows chattered high above the trees and decorated the pale sky with their swirling signature.

'How big is your father's farm?'

'This is his field, and the one next to it, and the one after that,' Edward answered. 'It will soon be harvest time and we will provide bread for the village.'

The man nodded. 'That is a fine way to use your time. And will you take over the farm from your father?'

'One day, these fields will be mine,' the boy said, looking out across the swaying heads. 'My family have always been farmers.'

'Then you and I have much in common,' the man said. 'A farmer sows seeds to feed the people. I sow ideas to feed their souls.' His smile was more convincing when he saw that Edward was confused. 'I am a holy man, child,' he continued. 'But my church is not made of stone and wood and lead. It is wherever I go.' He sat up straight in the saddle and raised his arms. 'Come to me,' he said, leaning down from the horse. 'I have something for you.'

Edward went over and the holy man gave him a book. It was heavy and smelt of its home in the leather saddlebag.

'This as well,' the man said, handing the boy a small wooden cross. 'Keep them close to your heart and follow where they lead,' he instructed, before tapping his heels against the horse and moving along the path. 'We all must eat to survive,' he said, raising his voice without turning to face Edward, 'but the key is finding what we need to live.'

It had been two hours since the man had left and Edward continued to think about their encounter. He sat cross-legged in the field, playing with the grains, watching them fall through his fingers into the dust.

I sow ideas to feed the soul.

He traced the last bit of corn as it fell to the earth before getting to his feet and tilting his head to enjoy the soft breeze on his face. A faint moon started to show above the trees. He imagined the field of corn as thousands upon thousands of tiny ideas waiting to germinate and transform the world. Edward was struck by the majesty of the image.

By the time he heard his mother calling him home for tea, he knew that he would not take over the farm from his father. He walked along the path and back towards their cottage. The late-afternoon sun shone through the branches of an overhanging tree and bathed the scene in a warm honey glow.

Edward hung the cross the holy man had given him from the headboard of his bed. When it was time to sleep, he felt happy knowing it was watching over him. He kept the book on his bedside table. He didn't open it immediately because he assumed it was a Bible like the one he read with his mother.

One morning, he woke early and, as his eyes adjusted to the light from the window, he saw how the dust in the room hung above the book like a genie emerging from a bottle. He reached over and pulled the book towards him, using both hands to lift it onto his chest. He lifted the hard leather cover and thought it smelt old. The language within was different to that of the Bible but shared the same authoritative tone. It spoke of the beginning of time and the creation of man and beasts, of plants and trees, of deserts, mountains, rivers and seas, and it did so poetically. An unusual rhyme gave certain sections the feeling of an incantation. Those stanzas were reserved for prophecies and their distinct metre helped commit them to memory. As Edward turned the pages, he read about times of turmoil and anxiety followed by periods of hope and happiness. Every story, good or bad, ended with a portent of change.

Noticing a fine ribbon used to bookmark the pages, he held it between thumb and forefinger and pulled. At first, he thought it lay inside the back cover, but then he saw that it marked the final few pages. He let the heavy front part of the book fall onto his thigh and started to read. The closing chapter told of a tribe in the wilderness. They had left their homes in search of a better life but had become marooned, trapped in a hinterland between their old world and the new. The book spoke of a stranger who could guide them to salvation. A golden girl.

Edward closed it to think. If this was not the Bible, then why had the holy man given it to him? He wondered if it was sinful to read any more, then decided it could not be as it was a gift from a man of the church. He smiled and climbed out of bed. He looked forward to sharing news of his discovery with his parents and reading more of this mysterious book.

The monastery was several miles from the farm where Edward lived. The villagers said it had been there for a thousand years, despite the priest telling them that church documents showed that it had been built in the early fifteenth century. Hundreds of years later, the monks came to the village to trade on the first Thursday of every month. Edward's father would give them corn for making bread, in return for beer and honey.

The monks took turns coming to the village, so Edward didn't get to know them apart from one who was in charge of the trading party. A squat, bald man with a white beard, who was unusually calm, and Edward liked him very much, making sure that he was there early each time the monks came to visit. The man's name was Brother Regis, and he would ask Edward what he'd been doing since they'd last met and if he was obeying his parents and respecting his elders. Edward was a mild-natured and well-mannered boy who was able to answer positively and truthfully. As they got to know each other, Edward would ask questions about the monastery and the life of a monk. Brother Regis saw that he was eager to learn and fed his interest with choice anecdotes.

One week, when Edward went to the market square with his father, the monk addressed them both and suggested to

Edward's father that it might be nice for the boy to visit the monastery. Despite his reluctance, Edward's father could see how much Edward wanted to go.

When they made the journey some days later, Edward was greeted by Regis, who showed him around while his father waited in the grounds. They were kept beautifully, with sculpted hedgerows and colourful flowers that attracted the bees. A large allotment provided food for the monks.

As Edward's father explored the gardens, he thought about his son's faith. He and his wife would pray on special occasions, such as the harvest festival, but Edward found spirituality in every aspect of daily life. His transformation had begun two summers ago, when he was playing in the big cornfield next to their cottage. His father had returned from putting the animals away for the night when the boy told him that he wanted to become a holy man. Over the following days, his parents had indulged the conversations about Edward's sudden conversion, but, as his resolve had strengthened and the weeks turned into months, then years, they'd realised that he was steadfast and his mind was set on leaving the farm. Much of his conviction stemmed from the book he had been given and his desire to understand its meaning. Eventually, their patience had worn thin when they were unable to change his mind. Edward was their only son and the farm had been in the family for many generations. If he refused to stay, they would need to try and persuade one of his cousins to take it over, or else the farm would be sold.

Leaning back now against the willow that overhung the lake in the grounds of the monastery, Edward's father thought back to the terrible row they had had one evening after dinner.

He and his wife had spent months, by this time, trying to change their son's mind about leaving the farm, while Edward had resorted to quoting passages from the book to justify his decision. On the night in question, he was reading it by the fire when his mother tried a different approach.

'Does your book tell you to forsake your family, Edward?' she asked.

He pretended not to hear her and continued reading.

'Answer your mother, boy!'

His father's voice made Edward jump and he quickly shut the book. He looked in shock from one to the other.

'I can feel your pain, Mother – yours too, Father – and I am sorry. It was not my intention to hurt you. This farm is your world, I understand that. You feel compelled to work here. But I do not. I have glimpsed another world beyond what we know and it draws me like a moth to this firelight,' he said, pointing.

'You have not answered my question, Edward,' his mother said. 'Does your book tell you to forsake your family?'

'No, it does not,' he replied. 'It says quite the opposite: that our family is more than those who simply live together under one roof. We have many brothers and sisters out there, lost, who need my help.'

Hearing this, Edward's father could contain his fury no longer and he snatched the book. Despite its weight, he lifted it above his head to cast it into the flames.

'You can burn the pages, Father, but not the ideas,' Edward said, refusing to look up at him.

'Not this way,' his mother urged, standing up and resting her arm on her husband's shoulder.

Edward's father had allowed the book to fall to the floor, sending a cloud of dust and ash into the air. The flames recoiled before they licked and bit at the particles, causing them to spit and glow as they went up the chimney. Edward picked up the book and returned to his chair, closed his eyes and hugged it to his chest.

The memory of that night was interrupted by the sound of a bell from the monastery. Its tone was comforting to hear and at one with the natural surroundings. It didn't disturb the birds or the animals, who continued singing and foraging for food. The monks were leaving the allotment and walking in single file up the hill. They reminded Edward's father of a line of cattle returning to the farm for the night. Two figures stood outside the building and waved to each other. One of them moved away against the flow of returning men. Edward's father saw his boy smiling and knew it must have been a good visit.

When Edward reached the lake, he told of what he had seen and learned, and what he must do to join the order. His father nodded and stroked the boy's head as they turned to go home. He wondered how he would have behaved at that age. When he was young, he had only wanted to go fishing and help his father on the farm. He would never have dared venture somewhere as unfamiliar and imposing as the monastery.

Walking back to the village, the trees that ran alongside the track cast long shadows across their path. Pigeons sighed in the branches and the light burnt to amber. Edward was unusually quiet, but his father understood. He was a serious boy who would be thinking about what life now held in store for him. There would be no more games and chasing his friends around the village.

When they were in sight of the farmhouse, his father spoke. 'What will you tell your mother?'

Edward continued to walk and study the ground in front of him.

'Edward?'

Edward stopped and looked at his father.

'I asked what you will tell your mother.'

'I will tell her I love her very much. I will also tell her I must leave our home to be closer to God.' Edward began walking again. 'You and Mother have brought me up with great tenderness and love, and shown me the good that shines in all things. I want to study that and understand it better, so I can show others.'

His father shook his head and laughed.

'What have I said?'

'Nothing, Edward. Your words show a mind far more attuned to the world than mine. I am proud of you,' his father said, giving him a playful push down the path.

Edward looked up as the last rays of the sun moved across his face.

*

When he turned fifteen years old, Edward arrived at the abbey and took the book with him. Although it was forbidden to bring possessions, he had discussed it at the market many times with Brother Regis. The monk had told Edward that he would enjoy reading it himself and that it would be a fine addition to their library.

Edward's first few weeks at the monastery were hard. He missed playing with his friends and found it uncomfortable spending long periods of time in silence. At night when he was in his cell, he missed his parents, and particularly his mother, who would hug him before he went to bed. He prayed for guidance and tried to put thoughts of his old life out of his mind. He believed that there was a purpose to his joining the monastery and was sure that he would adapt to its regime with time. Regis continued to play a key role in his life, teaching him the ways of the order. To begin with, this involved memorising the daily timetable and understanding when he was allowed to speak and how to address the other monks.

Before long, summer faded into autumn. The nights drew in and the weather turned cold. Occasional fires provided the only source of heat, and Edward's traditional habit and cloak were barely adequate against the bitter night-time temperatures and the sharp draughts that swept under the door of his cell. His homesickness improved, but his first winter at the monastery made him remember being back on the farm with his mother and father, lying with the dog in front of the fire. The memories made him smile and Edward learned to comfort himself by using his imagination to visit happier times.

One evening, after the monks had eaten and before prayers, Regis invited Edward to one of the reading rooms. The older man was pleased with how Edward was enduring a particularly harsh winter so early in his life at the monastery. 'Edward, in the room next to us are thousands of books; some so old that we cannot be sure exactly when they were written. But can you tell me which is the most valuable?'

The answer was so obvious that Edward thought there must be a catch. 'The Book of Our Lord,' he replied.

The monk nodded and, as he did so, Edward noticed how the lump in the older man's throat disappeared into a roll of fat. 'You are quite right, of course,' he said. 'It teaches us his values and enriches our lives. But we have many different versions, written by many disciples and scholars and monks down the centuries. So while it remains valuable spiritually, we are not bound to one volume.'

Edward tried to follow the clues.

Brother Regis got up and walked to a shelf above the desk in the corner of the room. He reached for a book that was so frequently handled it looked as if its leather dust jacket had been polished. It was Edward's book. The monk returned to his seat and let the book rest on his legs. 'There are some here who believe this should be destroyed; that we should use it to light the fire,' he said, before laughing. 'And on nights like this, I have some sympathy.'

Edward laughed too, happy to break his silence.

'But in all seriousness, the book divides people because it is powerful.'

'In what way?' Edward asked.

'Its power lies in questioning what we know to be true,' Regis explained. 'We find our faith in the Bible because it speaks the words of Our Father. But this book also comes from an ancient time and speaks with great conviction.'

'So why does it divide people?' Edward asked.

'Because some believe its voice is not Our Lord's.'

TWO

Elizabeth and the Ferryman

It was a hot night. The kind that leaves you twisting and turning and wrestling with the pillows before kicking off the sheets and wondering how anyone could sleep. The girl stood at her bedroom window, looking for signs of life outside. The street light cast the scene in an amber glow. A fox sniffed a recycling bin before moving off in search of food.

Going downstairs for a glass of water, the girl passed her parents' bedroom and heard her father snoring. The refrigerator hummed as her bare feet touched the cold floor of the kitchen. She wished it was as cool in her bedroom. She bent down on her hands and knees, and pressed her flushed cheeks against the stone slabs.

The heatwave in London had lasted for several weeks and the bricks and concrete of the city gave off their own warmth when the sun went down. The family had extended the back of the house, so floor-to-ceiling glass doors looked out from the kitchen onto the lawn. The girl never felt comfortable when it was dark as she couldn't see what was out there. Now she could. Peeling her cheek off the floor, she stood up and pressed her nose against the glass. A soft light flickered between the leaves. On the other side of the garden was the river and the towpath. If it was a boat or a late-night cyclist, the light should be moving. She felt her heart beat and knew she would not be able to go back to sleep.

Pulling tight on her dressing gown cord, she slipped into her father's shoes by the door and stepped out into the soft night air. To keep quiet, she took exaggerated, slow-motion steps down the garden. Reaching the bushes, she stopped and squeezed her head through a gap in the branches, leaving behind a golden strand of hair. The light was brighter now and still not moving. It appeared to come from the middle of the river. Careful not to let the hinges on the garden gate give her away, she stepped out into the lane. Edging closer to the water, she saw that the light wasn't coming from the river. It was suspended in mid-air above the bank, in the grip of a man in shirtsleeves. He turned slowly and raised the light. It showed a weathered face with deep, dark lines.

'Are you wanting to cross?'

She froze, unsure what to do.

'The river,' he growled. 'Are you wanting to go to the other side?'

Before the girl could answer, laughter floated across the water. It was a woman's voice and it had a beautiful, melodic note, as if played by the right hand of a pianist.

'The party's starting. You should come now before it's too late,' the man said. To the side of him was a shelter. A sign showed daily high tide information and opening hours. The girl saw that it should be closed by now.

'Are you the ferryman?'

'I'm Lucas Mann. My family have been taking souls across this river for as long as anyone can remember.' He turned in his heavy boots and shuffled towards the river. The current was coming from upstream, right to left, at a slow, hypnotic rate.

Seeing her chance, she ran, imagining rough hands reaching for the collar of her dressing gown. She heard him snort and prayed she had enough of a head start to make it back to the garden. Reaching the gate, she pushed it open. Risking a glance over her shoulder, she couldn't see him. Trying to scream, she made only the faintest sound.

Tom Fairchild had meant to replace the fridge for some time. His wife, Mary, complained about the noise and it irritated him that it would never shut the first time. It particularly bothered him that he was now battling to close it in the middle of another muggy, sleepless night after coming downstairs for some water. Finishing his drink, he felt a draught on his face. The windows were shut, so he went to check the back door and found it had not been closed properly.

If she could get across the garden, she was safe. The strength was draining out of her legs. The thought of the ferryman cutting off her escape made her feel sick. She turned quickly and collided with a man's hard body. His face was angry.

'Elizabeth! What on earth are you doing out here?'

She cried, then threw her arms around him and squeezed hard to be sure it really was her father. Remembering her pursuer, she flinched and checked again over her shoulder.

'Let's get you inside,' Tom said. 'We need to talk.' He put his arm around her and walked her to the back door. Locking it behind them, he stooped slightly to her height. 'What do you think you're playing at, leaving the house at this time of night?'

She hung her head to think. 'I didn't mean to. I was hot and couldn't sleep, and needed a drink. Then I saw a light outside and didn't know what it was.'

Holding her by the shoulders, he leant towards her and said, 'So you decided to unlock the back door and wander off?'

She couldn't tell him that a stranger had tried to take her out on the river. Her parents had instilled in her the importance of staying safe. Her father, in particular, worried whenever she was away from the house for any length of time and could get angry. 'I'm sorry, but I think I might have been dreaming. Sleepwalking. I'm really tired. Can I go back to bed now?' Sensing her moment, she reached up and kissed him on the cheek before slipping out of the kitchen and up the stairs.

Back in her bedroom, she listened to make sure he hadn't followed her, then went to the window, pulling aside one of the curtains, and looked out onto the garden. There was no sign of the light, but she thought she could make out the silhouette of a man in a rowing boat, heading for the far bank of the river.

They were unsure how Elizabeth had got her distinctive hair. When she was out of earshot, Tom would tease Mary about previous boyfriends, although they both agreed that their daughter's dark brown eyes came from Mary's mother,

Xena, who was born in Athens. Mary had grown up in England after Xena had met Mary's father in London while on holiday and never returned.

Hearing the language as she grew up had led Mary to read Greek at university, which was where she'd met Tom, who was giving a lecture on how the heavens were plotted during the Hellenistic period. The two became inseparable, although it took nearly ten years before Elizabeth was born. Before then, Mary had had her own career as a museum curator. She had planned to return to work once Elizabeth started school, then never got round to it. By that time Tom's career was on an upward trajectory, with research papers, books, and the occasional media appearance all supplementing his academic teaching, and they didn't need the money from a second salary.

Now in her early forties, and some years younger than her husband, Mary Fairchild was tall with an athletic figure and an infectious sense of humour that made her popular with several of the fathers on the school run. She was also the rock on which her family was built, providing encouragement and support for her husband's career while taking care of domestic duties and guiding Elizabeth through the emotional and academic travails of school life. With Elizabeth beginning to branch out socially on her own, Mary was looking forward to returning to work and the opportunity to throw herself into a fresh challenge.

Tom Fairchild had changed little since Mary had first met him nearly twenty-five years ago. He still wore baggy jumpers and cords with loafers, and had the same wavy, unkempt hair, albeit a little thinner now on top. His face now had laughter lines around his eyes, which Mary found ironic as he was usually serious unless Elizabeth was involved. The oversized sweaters also covered a growing paunch that was fed with fastidious regularity at the local pub. The bridge of his nose showed the indentation of heavy spectacles, and his index finger displayed the telltale yellow sign of a chain-smoker, despite him having given up the habit years earlier.

'What do you really think happened, Tom?' Mary sat opposite him at the kitchen table, nursing a hot drink.

He shook his head and raised his eyes to the heavens. 'Probably what she said,' he replied.

'Sleepwalking? I think that's unlikely, don't you? She's never done it before.'

'No, not that part. She probably did see something outside and go to investigate. You know what her imagination is like, Mary. I didn't see anyone else out there by the river.'

'I wonder what's triggered it?'

'Maybe something she's read or heard at school.' Tom rubbed his eyes and yawned. 'If we tread carefully around the subject tomorrow, we might be able to get something out of her.' He stood up and went over to the cupboard and reached for a glass.

'At this time of night, Tom?'

'Want one too?' He smiled, pouring himself a large whisky.

'I'm serious. Let's get back to bed and get some sleep.'

'I need a nightcap first. My nerves are shot,' he said, downing the drink. He went to the sink and rinsed the glass, then followed his wife upstairs.

THREE

The Ferryman

Lucas Mann had been a ferryman for more of his life than he had not and had never considered any other line of work. His family had run the river ferry for generations and there had been no question that he would do the same. It was as unavoidable as the tides that pulled and pushed his simple wooden craft across the great river, carrying passengers he didn't like. The water was his home and he could not imagine spending his time anywhere else. On the bank, with the passengers, he was irritable and distracted. Then when he stepped into his boat and pushed off, and the current lifted the bow and carried him towards the middle of the water, he was at peace. What he loved most was the smell: that dark, dirty odour that whips up your nostrils and fills your lungs.

On this night, it was particularly strong, thanks to a high tide that slopped at the sides of the boat and threw his passengers together. To hide their nerves, they laughed as they bumped shoulders. Lucas saw no humour in it and wished the idiots would keep quiet so he could enjoy the push and pull of the passage. When they had crossed, he allowed the side of the boat to hit the bank, causing them to cry out.

'Mann, you fool, you could've had us overboard.'

Lucas held the heavy oak oar in both hands and met the eyes of his accuser. The thought of retaliation made him smirk as the other man turned to climb out. Once the group was out of sight, Lucas sat back in the boat and thought once more of his mother. His father had never recovered from losing her and his behaviour had ensured the boy didn't either. All compassion, gentleness and affection in the house had died with her and been replaced by anger and resentment. Remembering those times, Lucas stood up and smashed the water with his oar, shattering the memories into a thousand glistening fragments.

'Why, Lucas, whatever seems to be the matter?'

He was startled and turned suddenly, nearly falling overboard.

The woman laughed. 'Careful there; you'll be no use to us without your boat.'

She was the only person he could tolerate laughing at him. The corner of his mouth twitched and he nodded. 'I'm not used to seeing you down here. You made me jump,' he replied.

The duchess laughed again and the last residue of anger drained out of him. She told him that they were expecting a special guest that he was to look after. A girl, accompanied by the woman's nephew, Tobias, who would be nervous making the crossing at night. Lucas nodded again.

'Lucas, I mean it.' She lowered her voice. 'I heard there was an incident with the last group.' She interrupted him when he tried to make an excuse. 'I don't want to hear it,' she snapped. 'We've had this discussion too many times. I know how much you like it down here on the river, Lucas,' she said, walking towards him. 'So don't do anything stupid to jeopardise it.' She lifted her mouth and blew softly in his face, before turning and walking away.

A light mist had come up from the middle of the river and rolled up and over the banks, creeping onto the towpath and into the fields. It quickly enveloped the duchess as she walked away.

After tea, Elizabeth was finding it hard to concentrate on her homework. Her mind kept returning to the events of the previous night. She wondered if the ferryman would be working again this evening. Later, in bed, she closed her eyes and imagined the guests preparing to go out. She thought about the lady with the musical laugh, and imagined she would have long dark hair and a beautiful, bright dress decorated with diamonds. Before long, she was asleep and the house creaked into place as the floorboards cooled and tightened.

In her dream, she was looking over the garden from upstairs at the back of the house. She was watching the ferryman and the light from his torch as it glinted across the black ripples of the river. A boy was standing beside him, wearing a man's shirt, with nothing on his feet. His hair was black, and when he turned to look up at the window, his face was as pale as his shirt. He smiled when he saw her.

She awoke with a start and sat up. Her breathing was fast and her face felt flushed. She kicked the covers off to cool down. Her mind was swimming from the dream, and she felt an urge to cross the landing and look out onto the garden. Her pulse thumped in her ears as she made her way to the rear of the house. Standing at the window, she looked down at the lawn and past the trees and the top of the ferryman's shelter. There was no sign of life.

At the end of the week, Elizabeth ran through the school gates, across the churchyard, and down the steps to the narrow lane alongside the river to her house. The route took her past the pub her father liked and the wooden hut that served as the ferryman's shelter. It looked as though the builder had run out of bricks for the walls and had to finish the upper part with the same type of wood they used for the roof. She was surprised how dilapidated it looked in daylight, with slats missing and a creeper devouring it. She poked her head inside and a spider's web caught her face. She shrieked, before wiping its sticky tentacles from her cheek.

'Everything all right, miss?' Lucas Mann filled the door frame.

'Oh… yes, I'm sorry. I didn't realise anyone was in.'

'I'm never far away. And tonight will be busy, with the ball at the big house. I don't want to miss no one.'

'There's another party?'

'Last week was more of a… dress rehearsal.'

She saw the same smile – the one she hadn't liked before – begin to play on his lips. 'Goodbye, then.' She turned for home and darted past him.

'See you later,' he replied.

She slowed but didn't look back. She knew he was still smiling.

That evening, they had a takeaway meal. It was Elizabeth's favourite, and she enjoyed watching her father try to eat with chopsticks before checking that her mother wasn't looking and shovelling the sticky food into his mouth with his fingers. Afterwards, they watched television and discussed their plans for the weekend. The weather remained warm and they decided it would be fun to hire a rowing boat and head upstream with a picnic.

Before long, the warm evening, the good food, and the beer he'd had after work cast their spell on Tom Fairchild and he fell asleep on the sofa. His wife and daughter didn't notice until his breathing grew faster and he began muttering, repeating the words 'Don't go.'

Mary rolled her eyes and looked at Elizabeth. 'I think it's time we all go up. Are you ready for bed?'

Elizabeth nodded. It had been a long week and the shock of bumping into the ferryman had left her exhausted. As she went upstairs, she looked forward to getting into bed and imagining what might be happening at the party later that night.

FOUR

The Lost Tribe

In her dream, Elizabeth heard a sharp tapping noise but didn't know where it was coming from. She woke up and opened her eyes. She was thinking about the dream when she heard the noise again.

Crack! Crack!

The clock by her bed showed 10pm. She sat up and stared at the window. Her body shook in time with the thumping in her chest.

Crack!

She didn't remember deciding to get out of bed, but found herself by the window with one hand on the curtain.

The noise again.

Elizabeth took a deep breath and nudged the corner of the fabric, making room to look out of the window. Keeping most of her face out of sight, she surveyed the scene with her left eye.

Crack!

She gasped. This time, the sound was so loud it made her ears ring. A piece of gravel cannoned off the windowpane in front of her nose. If this was a game, she didn't like it. She looked down to see who had thrown it. As her eyes grew accustomed to the low light, she saw movement by the tree across the road. She strained to focus before catching sight of a small figure moving behind the trunk. *What is he doing?* she thought, as he raised his arm to throw another stone. But instead his fist opened and he waved. It looked like the boy she had seen in her dream with the ferryman.

Elizabeth stepped back to make sure she wasn't dreaming again, then looked down the street to see if the boy was alone. She opened the window. 'What do you want?' she whispered.

He looked as if he hadn't heard.

'Who are you?' she asked.

He came closer, under the street light, and looked down, as if ashamed. She'd gripped the window handle to pull it shut when he looked up and stared at her with the bluest eyes she had ever seen. He smiled and waved again, motioning for her to come outside.

'Tell me who you are or I'm calling my parents.'

'I thought you wanted to come to the party?' he asked. 'The last boat leaves soon. You'll have to hurry.'

Elizabeth looked at her bed. It still showed the outline of where she'd been sleeping and the duvet she'd kicked off was now piled up on one side. She turned again to the window and looked to where the boy now stood motionless under a lamp post. She grabbed her clothes off the chair and got dressed. After straightening her hair in the mirror, she closed the front door with a soft click. 'How did you know where I live?'

'He told me,' the boy said.

'The ferryman?'

He nodded. 'He knows where everyone lives.'

'Is he there now?'

'He said you'd come but he won't wait long. We have to be quick.'

She thought about taking the shortcut through the garden, but couldn't risk disturbing her parents. That meant walking by the road instead. Before long, the breeze filled their heads with the earthy smell of the river. When they reached the bank, the ferryman stepped out from his shelter and went down the slope to the edge of the water. He used one hand to hold the stern of the boat, then put his foot in to steady it. Elizabeth carefully stepped over the side and sat down on the wooden plank that served as a seat. The boy took his place beside her, moving from the shore to the rocking boat. The ferryman grunted, pushed the boat out into the river, and stepped aboard. He pulled hard on the oars, taking them quickly into the middle of the water. The temperature dropped and the wind picked up, blowing Elizabeth's hair across her face. The water slurped and popped against the side of the boat as the oars cut deep into the current. The river had always looked safe and gentle from the footpath, so she was surprised by how it tugged at the small craft. Even in her father's inflatable, going across felt effortless. In the rowing boat, the ferryman had to aim higher up the bank to allow for natural drift to carry them to their landing point. Once there, he threw a rope around a wooden post and pulled to bring the boat close, allowing them to step off and climb up the steps to the footpath.

'The last boat goes at midnight,' he said.

'What if I'm late?' Elizabeth asked.

'You'll stay there.'

She chewed on her bottom lip. By now, the boy was already several yards ahead, so she ran after him.

'Did you pay him?' he asked when she caught up.

'No, should I have?'

'Don't worry about it.'

They carried on along the path and Elizabeth could smell the fields around them as the warmth of the day ebbed away.

'Have you been before? You know, to the party.'

'I live in the house,' he replied.

'Why were you on my side of the river, then?'

'I came to get you, of course,' he laughed.

It was true, she did want to go to the party, but she had no idea how Lucas Mann, the ferryman, would know that. 'Where exactly is it, anyway?'

'I'll show you,' the boy said. 'We need to go through the woods.'

They continued along the riverbank until they came to an iron gate cut into a stone wall. The boy squeezed past and they stepped into the woods. She noticed the temperature drop again, as it had on the boat, and the damp air tickled her nostrils when she breathed.

'It's cold in here. I don't like it.'

'Don't worry, it's warm in the house.'

'You still haven't told me your name,' she said.

He looked puzzled. 'My name is Tobias. Tobias Mallory.'

*

There were three moments that changed Edward's life forever. The first was when he was given the book in the cornfield. The second came one evening at the monastery. The monks were in bed, but he could not sleep. Moonlight passed through the stained-glass window and washed across the wall of the cell. It decorated the lime-and-sand plaster with pale-blue light. His mind turned to the book. It was rich in descriptions of the elements and the pull of the moon. Before long, he was in the library, reading by candlelight. He thought about the people who were lost. He wondered who they were and how many they numbered. What became of them? Did they ever find the golden girl and did she save them? Of course not – how could a girl be made of gold?

'Couldn't sleep either?'

Edward stood up.

'Please, sit down. You know, the older I get, the harder I find it to sleep, particularly when it's this light outside.' Regis sighed, pulling a stool over to the desk. He didn't have to ask what Edward was reading. Like mathematicians stuck on a cipher, over the years both men had become obsessed with Edward's book. 'What have you found?'

Edward shook his head. 'It's really nothing.'

'But...?'

'I've been thinking about the lost tribe.'

Regis gestured for him to continue.

'What if there was more than one tribe and what if there really is a girl who can save them, if we only know where to look for her?'

When Regis breathed, Edward heard the fabric of his habit scratch on his shoulders. He expelled the air slowly. '*We*, Edward?'

Edward was heading into dangerous waters. 'It is our shared belief that the book is both a historical document and an allegorical narrative,' he replied, as Regis nodded in agreement. 'What if it also tells of the future?'

The older monk brought his hands together in prayer and closed his eyes.

'Brother Regis?'

Regis answered after a long pause. 'Do you remember when I brought you into this library and we spoke of the value of your book?'

Edward nodded.

'Then you will also recall that I told you that some believe its words are not those of Our Lord.'

Edward went to speak but, with his eyes still closed, Regis raised his hand to stop him.

'I'm sorry, Edward, you must let me finish. If it is not his voice, then it cannot know what is yet to come.'

Edward accepted that the future was known only to God. But how could they be sure who was the book's author? If it came from the Lord, then the golden girl could be found. He decided he would have to pursue this theory alone. That was, unless he could convince some of the other brothers of the value of his idea.

He closed the book and wished Regis a good night. The book that had brought him to the monastery was now taking him in another direction. He needed to know more about the girl. He knew the book was old. It was also prophetic, yet it gave no timeline to events. She could have been guiding lost souls a millennium ago. She could also be among them now. Edward had to find out.

*

The path through Nightshade Wood snaked through the bushes and trees and was difficult to navigate. Everywhere was overgrown and there was little light, so Elizabeth stayed close to the boy. Occasionally, a branch snagged on her clothes and she pulled free. Among the trees, it was dark and cold and eerily silent. She imagined the guests arriving now, chattering with excitement. Then a clatter and movement out of the corner of her eye snapped her out of it.

'What was that?'

Neither of them moved as they tried to focus on where it had come from.

'A bird, maybe, clapping its wings in the branches,' Tobias said. 'It's nothing.'

Still unconvinced, she followed him as he continued on the path, looking over her shoulder as she went. 'What sort of bird? Crows or pigeons don't make that much noise, do they?'

'Maybe an owl.'

'Aren't owls silent hunters?'

'I don't know, then. But if it was after us, it wouldn't make that much noise, would it?'

He had a point, although the idea of something hunting them alarmed her. As they walked away there was another disturbance in the branches of a tree that towered above the rest. They didn't hear it this time. Nor did they see the eyes that glowed, following their progress.

When they reached a clearing, they heard voices. In front of them, a gravel drive led to a house cast in a faint white light from the moon.

'I take it this is where the party is?' she asked.

Tobias nodded.

'I wish I had something fun to wear,' she laughed, looking at the guests.

'Don't worry; we're not going in with them. I know a better way.'

He led her along the side of a hedge made of yew. When it reached the house, she stopped to look at a statue in front of the main doors. It was twice the size of a man and had a beard that hung from its chin down to its chest. The giant wore a crown of leaves and twigs, and lay across a stone plinth the size of a small car.

'Is that Neptune?'

'Father Thames,' he replied.

'And who is he exactly?'

'The god of the river, of course. Since Roman times, people have prayed to the river for food and transport.'

The boy then ducked behind the hedge and headed towards the rear of the house. Elizabeth stepped closer to the statue and saw an image of the moon engraved on one arm. She reached out to touch it, then quickly turned her head when she heard a noise behind her. Seeing nothing, she turned back to the statue, which had stepped off its plinth and stood before her. She screamed and ran in the direction the boy had taken. When she found him by the far corner of the building, he asked what had happened. He looked confused and asked her to show him. They crept back to where the stone statue continued to occupy its seat overlooking the river, as it had done for centuries.

'Are you all right, Elizabeth?'

'I told you I saw him stand up!'

Tobias decided to change the subject. 'Come on, I'll show you where they bring the food for the kitchen,' he said.

There were six steps up to the side of the house, with a metal handrail on either side. The grey slabs of stone bowed in the middle from all the footsteps down the years that had rubbed them smooth. Elizabeth followed Tobias up to the door. Inside, the hallway was dark. Coats hung on wall pegs and shoes were on the floor.

'This is just the boot room,' he explained. 'That door leads to the kitchen. This one will take us to the library.'

She noticed the musty smell of old hardback books. Every wall was covered in shelves and packed with more books than she had ever seen. They were stacked tightly together, apart from a single volume that was missing directly in front of her. The break in symmetry bothered her. 'Tobias,' she whispered. '*Tobias!*' A little more forcefully this time.

He stopped at the far end of the library.

'There's one missing,' she said. 'Look.'

Before she could say any more, he reached for the corner of the bookcase and gave it a firm shove. Rows of books started to move as the panel opened. When it was wide enough, he stepped sideways through the gap, beckoning for her to do the same. Checking to see if anyone was watching, she stepped into the cavity behind the wall. There was a soft rasping noise as the door closed behind them. It was pitch black. Her mouth was dry and she felt short of breath.

'Where are you? I'm scared.'

There was a scratching noise and the catacomb burst into light.

'Hello.' He smiled, holding a candle to his face. 'Let's go and join the party.'

Music drifted through the corridors like cigarette smoke towards an open window. The pair emerged from a passage into an entrance hall with portraits on the walls and suits of armour guarding a fireplace that crackled and glowed from a pyramid of burning logs. She could hear the sounds of instruments coming from the other side of the arched doors across the hall. As a new group of guests entered, there was a burst of noise and excitement. The hall was filled with colour and commotion as men and women swept across the polished wooden floorboards, shiny shoes clip-clopping in time with their voices. None of them looked at Elizabeth or Tobias. The pair turned to each other and laughed. Without saying a word, they followed the partygoers into the main room before the doors closed. Couples waltzed across the floor and the ceiling glistened with thousands of tiny stars from the candlelight of golden chandeliers.

'I feel like Cinderella,' Elizabeth gasped.

'Who?'

She laughed.

'Aren't you going to introduce me to your friend, Tobias?' A woman with diamonds in her hair stood in front of them, as upright as a ballet dancer. She looked at Elizabeth.

'My name's Elizabeth Fairchild. Are you Tobias's mother?'

The woman lifted her exquisite chin and laughed. The sound was like raindrops on wine glasses; quavers and minims dancing together in honeycombed harmony. Elizabeth recognised the laugh from when she was by the river with the ferryman. 'I'm not his mother. I am the duchess, but you can call me Gabriella. Why don't you take my arm and I'll introduce you to our friends?'

The room fell silent. The musicians stopped and the

dancers stepped away from their partners to watch. There was a gentle swoosh as a sheet of music slipped off a stand and see-sawed to the floor. Elizabeth noticed the duchess looking at her hair and felt her tease its golden strands through her fingers.

'Gabriella? I believe you were about to make an introduction.' The man had a thin moustache, a square chin, and pale-green eyes.

'Forgive me – I was lost in thought,' the duchess replied. 'Ladies and gentlemen, we have a special guest tonight. A friend of Tobias. May I introduce Elizabeth Fairchild.'

There was a polite round of applause and Elizabeth blushed. She turned to Tobias, who kept his head down.

'Come on, darling, don't leave the child standing there. Elizabeth, let me show you around. I'm the duke, Charles Featherstone, and Gabriella's husband.' The man with the lupine eyes tilted his head and smiled.

Elizabeth did as he asked, glancing at Tobias, who ignored her. As the duke moved among his guests with her, the musicians picked up their instruments and resumed playing.

An old man entered the room, carrying a large book. He had a heavy limp that caused his long white hair to swing from side to side. His nose was angled like an insect's leg and a pair of round spectacles perched where the foreleg met the thigh. 'I have it – it's here!' he exclaimed.

Charles looked at the duchess, who moved to cut the man off.

'Not now, Solomon, please.' She smiled. 'Shall we go back to the library and take a look?'

The librarian refused, so they moved to a table at the far

end of the room. 'It's here, I tell you,' he hissed, prodding at the page.

Gabriella leant in to take a closer look. They both then glanced at Elizabeth before returning to the book. After the librarian had left the room, the duchess went to find her husband.

'Charles, may I have a word?'

He moved away from Elizabeth, reluctantly.

Tobias went over to Elizabeth. 'You have to come with me quickly,' he said.

She saw the concern in his eyes and followed him to the door. After he turned the handle, a man's hand slammed it shut.

'Where do you think you're going?' A guest stood between them and the door.

'The duke said we could go,' Tobias said.

The man turned to look at Charles, giving Elizabeth and Tobias the opportunity to squeeze past and into the hallway. They ran until they reached the end of the corridor and a door underneath an ancestral painting. It was locked. Tobias banged his fist on the wood.

'Who's there?'

The children looked at each other in surprise.

'It's me, Tobias. Let me in.'

Elizabeth looked over her shoulder and saw the man who had blocked their path lumbering towards them before being overtaken by two younger men. All three were shouting for her and Tobias to come back. There was a heavy clunk as the key turned in the door and the librarian's beak-like nose appeared. Before he could speak, Tobias pushed past, with Elizabeth close behind. The boy led the way to a section of wood panelling and shoved it with his shoulder.

'What are you doing?' shrieked Solomon.

As the door shut behind them, they heard their pursuers enter the library.

'If we don't light a candle, they can't follow,' whispered Tobias. 'I know where I'm going. They don't.'

It was dark. The boy led the way and Elizabeth followed closely. She didn't remember the passageway being this long and imagined all sorts of horrors waiting in the dark.

'Tobias, why are they chasing us?' She closed her mouth when a sticky, fibrous mesh covered her face. Her eyelashes were glued together and tiny legs crawled across her cheek. She screamed.

'Shh – you must not make a sound or they'll know where we are,' he hissed. 'It's only a spider's web. Stay close; it's not much further.'

The men heard her scream and began shouting and crashing down the corridor. She put her hand in front of her face as the passageway lit up. Tobias had found the door and light flooded in from the kitchen.

'Quick,' he said, ushering her through the gap before closing the door. He ran over to a wooden stool and jammed the seat under a horizontal panel in the hidden door.

When they got outside, it was another cloudless night and a clear moon held dominion over a black universe. A pair of red eyes watched them approach from the cover of the trees. The first thing Elizabeth noticed when they got outside was the smell of the flowers. The scent of sherbet roses and lemon jasmine hung in the air. She filled her lungs with their perfume and ran after Tobias down the stone steps at the side of the house towards the gardens. When they reached a tall, thick hedge made of yew, he glanced back at her.

'Come on, this way,' he urged, guiding her round the back of the hedge.

'Where are we going?'

'Somewhere they'll never find us.'

The wall of yew was now either side of them and it was harder to see where they were. The boy seemed to be taking random turns – left and right, then right again, then left – disorientating her.

'Please tell me you know where we're going.'

'I told you; I know a place where they'll never find us. They don't bother coming in here any more as they always get lost.'

As they headed further into the maze, they heard voices coming from the house.

'Where are they?'

'If that boy has taken her, there will be hell to pay.'

'They're probably just playing.'

'Tobias, where are you? Come out and show yourself.'

Elizabeth froze and looked at him.

'Don't stop!' he urged.

When they reached the centre of the labyrinth, he stopped running.

'Now what?' she asked, her voice breaking. 'We're trapped, aren't we?'

The voices sounded closer. There was the crack of a cane on the hedge as one of their pursuers hit out in frustration.

The boy smiled. 'Sounds like someone's lost.'

Elizabeth began to panic and looked for an escape route.

Tobias put his hands up to calm her. 'Don't make a noise and they won't find us. They have never reached the end of the maze.'

The boarding school had stood in a corner of lush English countryside for close on a thousand years. Starting life in the Renaissance under the direction of a local abbey, the school had produced world leaders, captains of industry, war heroes, and more than its fair share of miscreants who had scandalised society down the years. It had also educated and spat out Tom Fairchild.

The early years of his childhood had been idyllic and unremarkable. He'd attended a nearby primary school with several children he had known since he was born, and the holidays were spent playing with them in the local playgrounds and at their houses. That changed when Tom turned seven and his parents decided to spend their life savings on giving him a private education. Removing him from the network of friends he had grown up with was unsettling, but the real trauma was being separated from his parents. There wasn't a day that went by at boarding school when he didn't wish with every particle of his body that he was back at home. The holidays passed in the blink of an eye, while term time stretched into an eternity spent navigating the mood swings of bullying older boys and the occasional violent teacher. The years away from his family had scarred Tom and instilled in him a deep insecurity and fear of losing those he loved.

Forty years later, Tom was in bed beside Mary when the sound of milk bottles in the street woke them. He had opened the window earlier in the day and now Mary was reminding him that she'd asked him to close it before they went to bed. He sighed and got out of bed. He saw the milkman picking up the bottles he had knocked over and quietly cursed him, wondering why the milk was now delivered late at night instead of in the morning.

'There's no need for that sort of language either,' Mary said, causing Tom to use some more.

After closing the window, he remembered he'd left Elizabeth's open. He decided to go and shut that too before she was disturbed. Her room was dark and he could smell the night air from the open window. On the far side of the bed, he saw her body-shaped duvet. He closed the window, then crept towards the bed to bend down and kiss her.

The air left his lungs. His daughter was gone and the bed where she'd lain was cold. She had been missing for some time.

Elizabeth shrieked. A hand came through the hedge by her head. In front of them, a carved stone marked the centre of the maze. Tobias ran forward and used it as a step to jump onto the top of the hedge. In one movement, he sat down on the crest of the foliage, then disappeared.

'Tobias!' She knew she couldn't jump that high, so she had to pull herself up. When she stood up on the plinth, she felt exposed and vulnerable. The muscles in her arms burned and tingled from the effort. There was a rustle in the hedge behind her and she screamed again, imagining Solomon's claws reaching for her. She threw herself forward and her feet disappeared into the upper part of the hedge as she grabbed for a handhold. Eventually, she rolled her body across the top of the hedge and was able to reach the other side before dropping to the ground. Crouching, she looked up at the boy.

'Don't worry,' he said. 'We really are safe now. Follow me.'

Leaving the maze, they arrived at the perimeter of the kitchen garden. There was just enough light for them to make their way past the house and back to the woods. When they reached the trees, Tobias crouched behind a tangle of brambles thick with nettles. Elizabeth joined him and squatted on her haunches, trying to catch her breath.

'Why are we stopping?' she said.

'Once they've found their way out of the maze, I don't think they'll come into the woods, but I can't be sure.'

'Then why not keep running?'

'Because then we won't know when it's safe to stop,' he said.

She shook her head in frustration.

After waiting a few minutes, he stood up. 'They're not coming.'

Elizabeth remained wary and stayed down behind a bush. 'Are you really sure?'

'We would've seen them by now.' He stepped over a dead branch and started to walk along the path back towards the river.

'Why didn't they follow us into the woods?'

'They prefer it inside,' he said, continuing to walk. 'Some people think the woods are dangerous at night and don't like to come here. And they also don't know their way around like I do.'

'Dangerous?' she asked, running to catch up with him.

'Aren't you afraid of the dark?'

'Grown-ups aren't scared of the dark, Tobias, just children.'

Before he could answer, someone else did. 'Everyone is scared of the dark.'

It made Elizabeth jump and the ferryman laughed. The gentle slap of water on a boat's hull drew her gaze to the reeds and she saw the faint outline of his boat. Its oars rested in their rowlocks, tucked in and pointing backwards.

'I wasn't sure you were coming. It's getting late,' he said. 'This will be the last trip tonight.'

She followed him down the bank, grabbing fistfuls of reeds to keep her balance, and stepped aboard. 'Tobias, I'm not sure what just happened tonight,' she said, looking up to where he stood on the towpath.

'I can explain another time, but you must go now.'

'When will I see you again?'

The ferryman snorted and cleared his throat before spitting downstream. Elizabeth looked back at the boy, who was staring at the moon that had reappeared from behind a cloud.

'I will come and see you again soon,' he said.

She sat down on the bench in the boat and Lucas Mann began to pull against the current. She tried to make herself comfortable and watched the strange boy, who remained transfixed by the moon – its soft light adding a waxy complexion to his pale skin.

Mary heard Tom call Elizabeth's name before he burst into their bedroom and turned on the light.

'Where is she, Tom?'

'I've no idea, but the bed's cold, which means she's probably been out half the night.' He pulled on a pair of jeans and grabbed a T-shirt from the drawer.

She followed him downstairs in a dressing gown, clutching her phone. 'Shall I call the police?'

'Let's get outside first and see if she's down by the river again. If she's not, then call them,' he said, unlocking the back door and running barefoot into the garden.

Mary had goosebumps hearing him shouting for Elizabeth. He was out of sight quickly, having vaulted the gate at the end of the garden and headed for the water. He called Elizabeth again and then Mary heard him gasp. She fumbled with the phone as she ran, trying to key in the numbers for the emergency services. When she was fifty yards short of the old ferryman's hut, she saw her husband shaking. Speaking to the operator as she ran, she then dropped the phone, smashing it on the footpath, when she saw Elizabeth in Tom's arms.

'Tom, is she…?'

'She's fine, Mary. Bloody stupid, and in a whole world of trouble with her parents, but she's fine.'

Elizabeth looked at Mary and then pushed her face into her father's shoulder to hide her shame.

FIVE
—

I Saw You in My Dreams

That night, Elizabeth fell into a sleep so deep she barely moved. Dreams came quickly, filled with images of dark figures in cloaks with shining eyes and lizard tongues. Her pulse raced and she began sweating.

In the bedroom below, Mary had finally fallen asleep after the earlier drama, her body turned towards the wall. Tom was unable to unwind and was propped up against the headboard, with a small reading torch clipped to a file of research papers. His concentration was broken by talking. He raised his head and took off his glasses, sitting motionless, trying to hear where it was coming from. The voice again. A woman's and she sounded upset. He shifted his weight to the side of the bed and got up carefully, so as not to disturb Mary. He went to the window and looked into the garden. The security light at the back of the house had not gone off, so if the voice wasn't coming from outside, that meant it was inside his home.

He went for the bedroom door. Out on the landing, he stopped to listen again. The voice was louder now and coming from the floor above. He shouted to wake Mary, then ran, taking the stairs two at a time. Outside Elizabeth's door, he realised that the woman's voice was actually his daughter's, although it sounded different. Between sobs, she was calling out for someone and she was now making a noise like a wounded animal. He opened the door and turned on the light. Elizabeth was on her back and the outline of her body was rigid. Only her lips were moving. When he approached, he saw a bead of sweat move across her forehead and roll down her temple.

'Elizabeth, are you all right?'

She didn't respond, but started to take short, sharp breaths.

'Tom, what is it?' Mary stood behind him. 'What's happening?'

'She's having a nightmare. I heard her crying out in her sleep. She could have a fever.'

'Tobias, he's behind you – run!' Elizabeth shouted. 'No! Don't touch him. Leave him alone,' she mewled.

Tom approached the bed and put his hands on her shoulders. 'Elizabeth, it's Daddy. You're having a nightmare. Wake up, sweetheart.'

She turned her head towards him. Her eyes remained closed. Her hair was wet against her skin and he wiped it from her face.

'Tom, do you think she's all right?' Mary asked, stroking her daughter's cheek.

They pulled back the duvet and he wrapped both arms under Elizabeth, lifting her into a sitting position.

'Elizabeth, wake up now! Elizabeth!' He shook her and she let out a sigh. A trace of saliva appeared at the corner of her mouth and started to slip over her bottom lip. He caught it with his index finger and wiped it on the bed sheet.

'Darling, it's Mummy and Daddy. You're just having a nightmare. Time to wake up,' Mary implored.

The girl's head rolled back slightly and her eyes began to open. She was struggling to focus. 'Dad?' She leant forward and put her arms around his neck. 'I had the most terrible dream.'

'I know you did, baby, but it was just a dream and we're here now,' he said.

She pulled away from him and turned to Mary. 'I can't believe I'm awake, Mummy. I was so sure it was real.'

'Why don't you tell your mother all about it, while I go and get you a flannel to cool you down?' Tom said.

When he was out of the room, Mary gave a weak smile. 'Come on, then – tell me all about it,' she said.

Elizabeth went to speak, then stopped. She looked confused.

'What is it?'

'It's kind of weird,' Elizabeth replied. 'Everything was so clear a moment ago and now I can't remember anything at all.'

'Well, I might be able to help with that,' Mary said. 'You were calling out for someone. Tobias, I think you said.'

There was a flicker of recognition in Elizabeth's face, which made her answer all the more surprising. 'No, I don't remember a Tobias,' she said quietly.

The pair looked into each other's eyes.

'Well, it doesn't matter,' Mary said. 'The spell is broken and you're awake now. How are you feeling?'

Tom came back into the room and laid a damp cloth on Elizabeth's forehead.

'I'm fine now, honestly. Perhaps I'll remember what the dream was about in the morning,' she said.

'Don't worry about that,' Tom reassured her. 'Try and forget about tonight and just get some sleep.'

They both bent down and kissed her on the cheek before leaving the room. When they were gone, she lay on her back and chewed the corner of her lip. She was trying to decipher the dream and whether it could be a portent. It was so vivid she could still smell the vegetation of the woods and hear the twigs crack underfoot. The moment she shut her eyes, she was back in the dream again. It was too intense to resist. She walked along the path and saw a piano in a clearing between the trees. The unlikely juxtaposition unnerved her and she started to perspire. The fallboard on the piano was raised, exposing the keys, ready for someone to play. She put her arm out for Tobias. As she did, a single clear note rang out from the piano. She could see that one of the ivory keys had been pressed and the sound pierced the damp night air as clearly as the edge of a knife hitting a wine glass.

'Everything OK?' Her father's voice dispelled the image and she breathed again. He had come back in to check on her.

'I was trying to remember the dream and I think I must've drifted off. I'm sorry if I disturbed you.'

'I actually thought you were playing music in here. I heard the sound of a piano,' he said, watching the blood drain from her face. 'Are you sure you're OK, darling? You look pale.'

'Dad, I heard the same thing,' she said, studying his face for a reaction.

He smiled and walked over and put his hand on her

head. 'You're hot.' He went to the bathroom and returned with a thermometer that confirmed she had a fever. 'I'll be back in a moment.'

She felt cold and brought her knees up to her chest to keep warm. When he returned with a glass of water and painkillers, she was asleep. He put them on her bedside table and returned to his room.

The next day was Saturday, and Mary and Tom let Elizabeth sleep in. When she got up, the fever was gone, along with all memory of what had happened the previous evening. They sat her down and explained that if she told them why she had left the house at night, she wouldn't be in trouble. She said that all she could remember was going to bed and waking after a nightmare.

'Why aren't you telling us the truth?' Tom demanded, getting annoyed.

'I am!' she protested, looking at Mary and starting to cry.

'Tom, I think she's telling the truth. She did have a fever, remember?'

He sighed. 'Don't cry, sweetheart, it's OK,' he said, pulling Elizabeth to his chest. 'Your mother could be right. You picked up a little bug and were a bit delirious last night.' He lifted his shirt and dried her tears.

*

The journey there had been easy. David Montague took an early train from Paddington, arriving in Exeter before 9am. He called in at the village shop to buy his mother some flowers and a newspaper, and told Mrs Clyde behind the counter how well she looked. He'd grown up in the village and was always surprised by how she never seemed to change. He imagined she would have made the perfect farmer's wife, with her rosy cheeks and her hair pulled tight into a brown bun. Mrs Clyde told him that his mother had called into the shop yesterday and was looking forward to his visit. As he left, he held the door for a long-haired teenager whom he vaguely recognised but couldn't quite place.

Mrs Montague lived in a thatched cottage by a lane that led to a small chapel. Three minutes later, Montague was at the bottom of the hill, carefully negotiating the icy path so as not to slip, and knocked on the door. He heard movement inside and shouted a greeting. The door opened and she hugged him. They went inside and he took his bags up to the spare room. When he returned, they had some shortbread with a pot of tea. As he was trying again to explain the difference between online and broadcast journalism – and why she hadn't seen him on television – it happened. His mother had raised a bone china cup to her mouth when there was a loud screech and a thump, followed by silence. The sound of protesting rubber and crumpled metal was unmistakable. Montague pushed his chair back and ran for the door.

At the entrance to the lane, his heart quickened. A tractor carrying straw bales had pulled out of the junction and been hit by a small hatchback that was now wedged underneath its trailer. The farmworker was leaning out of the tractor, looking down on the remains of the smaller vehicle. Montague approached the car and squeezed his head and shoulders through the gap where the passenger window had been. There was a bloody imprint on the inside of the windshield. The driver was unconscious with his head resting on the steering wheel. Montague called out but got no reply. Reaching deeper into the car, he hooked his forearms under the man's armpits and carefully started hauling him out of the seat. His mother, who had followed him out of the cottage, was now standing on the pavement, and told him that the emergency services were on their way. She knew the tractor driver and asked him what had happened.

'I didn't see him,' he said. 'I was just turning out of the lane and the next thing I know there's a bang and I look down and see the car, but it wasn't there when I pulled out.'

Montague tried to ignore him as he struggled to pull the man over the gearstick. *You didn't see it because you didn't look*, he thought, imagining how the tractor had pulled out onto the road without stopping, as it did, no doubt, every morning. The car driver was not wearing his seat belt and now lay unconscious at the side of the road, blood-matted hair stuck to the side of his face. Montague saw that it was the teenager from the shop. As the young man hung between life and death, he recognised the child who used to help his mother stock the shelves in the village store.

It was then that Mrs Clyde arrived on the scene. She was hysterical and calling for her 'baby boy'. Mrs Montague intercepted her and said to let her son, David, help him. After failing to find a pulse and pounding on the boy's chest, Montague tried mouth-to-mouth resuscitation. Eventually, he sat back on his heels, wiped his mouth, and hung his head. Mrs Clyde's wailing was accompanied by the noise of sirens. Montague knew Mrs Clyde's son was dead, but as the ambulance left the village, lights flashing, he found himself praying. He offered nothing in exchange; just a simple petition to anyone up there to deliver a miracle.

That evening, he ate a simple meal of roast chicken and salad with his mother, and said little until several glasses of wine had been drunk. She repeated that he had done everything he could and shouldn't blame himself. In truth, he didn't, but he did feel angry that he was unable to save the boy.

At the end of the night, he'd turned out the last light and started up the stairs when there was a knock at the door. Through the glass, he saw the slumped figure of a man leaning on the door frame. He released the deadbolt and turned the handle. The security chain stopped their visitor falling into the hallway. Montague put his hand on the man's chest and pushed him upright so he could unhook the chain.

The tractor driver smelt of beer and stale sweat. 'I need to speak to your mother,' he slurred.

Montague shook his head. 'It's late. If you have something to say, then tell me and I'll let her know in the morning.'

The man became aggressive and shouted about how the car had been going too fast and he hadn't seen him.

'You're a good man who was setting out on an honest day's work and meant no harm to anyone,' Montague said. 'Go to bed and get some rest. You'll feel better in the morning.' He closed the door and thanked God he wasn't in the other man's shoes. The same God he had prayed to earlier. *Twice in a day*, he thought to himself.

Over breakfast, Montague and his mother talked again about what had happened. As he was emptying the scraps off their plates, they heard the doorbell. He soaked the plates in hot water while she answered the door. After turning off the tap, he tried listening to what was being said. He had expected to hear the tractor driver again, but instead he heard a woman. After hearing his mother gasp, he went to investigate. She had her hand to her mouth and was shaking. As he reached out to hold her, she stepped forward and put her arms around the other woman. They were both crying and Montague saw that their visitor was Mrs Clyde.

'I'm so sorry, Mrs Clyde…' he began, stopping when he saw them smiling through their tears.

His mother spoke. 'He's alive, David.'

'What?!'

'He's on a ventilator but Marcel's alive,' Mrs Clyde explained. 'Despite breaking heaven knows how many bones, they say he's going to make it. The ambulance crew managed to get his heart going on the way to the hospital. They said someone up there must like him.' She laughed, before dissolving into tears once more.

'That's not possible.' Montague let the words hang in the air before tears of joy overcame him too.

After Mrs Clyde's son was discharged from hospital, she asked Montague if he would come and visit. Three months after he had prayed by the young man's body, unable to find a pulse, he was now looking into the eyes of a dead man. Marcel Clyde opened the front door and gave an embarrassed laugh before looking away. The silence was awkward.

Montague cleared his throat. 'You're looking well, Marcel,' he began. 'I thought we'd lost you.'

Marcel smiled without conviction, unable to find the right reply. Montague took a step forward and the men again looked at each other before suddenly embracing. They both seemed surprised, but the urge to connect physically was too strong.

'Looks like I need to put the kettle on,' Mrs Clyde laughed.

Montague smiled and Marcel led him into the sitting room. The young man limped over to an armchair and sat down. He had made incredible progress but the way he lowered himself into the chair showed his pain. After detailing his injuries, along with the various surgical procedures and physiotherapy sessions, Mrs Clyde came in with refreshments. As she poured their guest a cup of tea, she said, 'You know, we owe you so much. I was telling your mother only the other day that if it wasn't for your quick thinking, Marcel wouldn't be with us today.'

Montague had agreed to visit because he knew that his attempts to save the young man had failed. He actually wanted to apologise for not being able to do more, but he also needed to understand how Marcel Clyde was still alive. And if he was honest with himself, he wanted to see with his own eyes that the boy really was alive. 'That's very kind of you, Mrs Clyde. I only wish it were true.' He smiled. 'But my efforts at CPR failed to register a pulse.' Turning to Marcel, he said, 'When I left you lying in the road, you were dead.' Hearing the words, he was shocked at their brutality and regretted saying them. This was a family still traumatised by a terrible accident and he was making it worse.

Mrs Clyde got up and threw her arms around Montague's

neck, leaving a lipstick kiss on his cheek. 'That's for saving my boy's life and being too humble to admit it,' she said.

'The doctors said you giving me mouth-to-mouth provided just enough oxygen to keep my brain alive until the paramedics could hook me up to the ventilator in the ambulance,' Marcel explained.

Mrs Clyde tried again to make Montague understand. 'You may not have noticed any response, but you breathed life into my son,' she said, her voice trembling.

'You were dead, Marcel,' Montague said and shook his head. He stood in the sitting room, watching the sun disappear between the trees through the cross hairs of the leaded windows. He had seen death before. Marcel's explanation was plausible to a point, though no amount of CPR or mechanical ventilation could reanimate a corpse. Mother and son looked at him sympathetically, waiting for the penny to drop. He snorted. 'Are you suggesting there was some kind of divine intervention at work?'

Marcel laughed. 'As if.'

'There is no other explanation,' Montague continued, more forcefully than he'd intended.

'You can choose to believe whatever you like, David,' Mrs Clyde said.

Montague threw up his hands and then realised he was probably missing the point. Marcel and his mother didn't care what combination of science or divinity had saved him, so why should he? And whichever way you looked at it, Marcel's recovery was nothing short of miraculous. He smiled. 'You could be right, Mrs Clyde. Maybe the breath of the Lord did fill my lungs that morning.'

As the front door closed behind him and he set off on

foot towards his mother's home, Montague felt unsettled. He inhaled deeply to calm himself and let the warm air escape slowly from between his lips. On this damp evening, it created a mist that drifted upwards to the heavens.

'How did it go?' his mother asked, working at the kitchen sink. When he didn't reply, she turned around. 'David?'

Montague shook his head and laughed. 'Lazarus indeed has risen from the grave.'

'Well, you knew that before you went. Did he explain how they saved him?'

'He told me what they said to him in the hospital. It still doesn't make sense.'

'Then there can be only one explanation,' she said, passing him a glass of wine.

'Not you as well.' He lifted the drink to his lips.

She raised an eyebrow.

'In a world filled with tragedy, war, terrorism, sick children, and famine, you think the Almighty slipped a get-out-of-jail-free card to a kid who was driving too fast in your village?'

She remembered indignant outbursts like this from him when he was a child and was surprised to find he hadn't changed. 'No, David,' she said, raising her glass to him. 'The only explanation is that you were mistaken. Marcel Clyde was still with us when he was taken into the ambulance.'

That night, Montague was comforted by the sound of the old beams in the cottage settling in for the night, creaking and groaning as they contracted in the cold night air. An evening spent talking in front of an open fire followed by the bed he'd had as a boy usually sent him to sleep instantly. Not tonight. He couldn't stop thinking about the accident.

If he could agree with his mother and accept that he had been wrong, then he might sleep. She had not seen men die, though, and would not recognise the pallor of the face when life slips away.

After a fitful night, he contacted the hospital the next morning and asked to speak to the doctor who had treated Marcel Clyde. Half an hour later, Dr George Mason's assistant rang and told him that it was against hospital policy to discuss a patient. However, the doctor would meet him for a quick coffee at the end of the day as a thank-you for administering first aid at the scene of the crash. Montague took the back roads to the city hospital and thirty minutes later pulled into the car park just before 6pm. He went to the coffee shop by the reception and sat down with an espresso.

'You know that won't do your heart any good.'

He looked up to see a woman in her thirties, dressed in suit trousers and tennis shoes, smiling at him. The sleeves of her top were rolled up to the elbows and a stethoscope hung around her neck.

'Dr Mason?' he asked.

She laughed. 'Yes, I know. Georgina.'

They shook hands and he offered her a coffee.

'Better make mine a double espresso.'

They both laughed. She repeated again how patient confidentiality prevented her from discussing Marcel. She would, however, explain the science behind near-death experiences.

Montague finished his coffee and pushed the cup to one side. 'Fine. But he was dead, Dr Mason,' he said.

'I think what you really want to know is: at what point is someone dead?' she replied.

He nodded.

'Not very long ago, if there was no heartbeat, lung function or brain activity, you would be declared dead. But we now have the equipment to reverse those conditions occasionally,' she explained.

'Go on.'

'I have treated several patients who were technically dead, then came back from the brink.'

'Like Marcel,' Montague said.

She didn't reply.

'So at what point do you die?' he asked. 'When is it actually over and someone is beyond the point of resuscitation?'

'Probably after forty minutes of CPR. If there are still no vital signs, you can pretty much guarantee they're dead.'

'Forty *minutes*? On TV, you're lucky if you get forty seconds!' Montague shook his head. 'OK, so you won't tell me about Marcel,' he said. 'Then let's say, for argument's sake, someone suffered sudden, violent trauma in a road accident and failed to respond to attempts at resuscitation. They showed no vital signs and, quite frankly, appeared dead. What are the chances they could live?'

'It would depend on how long they had been unresponsive. Anything approaching forty minutes and the chances are pretty slim. Beyond that, you're getting into miracle territory.'

He thought back to the accident. How long had it been from hearing the crash to Marcel receiving treatment in the ambulance? It had taken Montague a minute to get out of the house and reach the scene of the accident, and then maybe seven or eight minutes to pull Marcel out of the wreck. If his mother had called the ambulance at that point, it was about ten minutes from the impact. 'Do you know how long it took the ambulance to respond to our 999 call?'

Dr Mason rolled her eyes and nodded. 'They took twenty-five minutes to reach the village.'

OK, that's thirty-five minutes and counting, he thought. 'And at what point did he respond to treatment?'

She shook her head. 'I'm sorry; that's confidential patient information.'

Montague gave a resigned smile and got up to leave. He shook hands with Dr Mason and thanked her for her time.

'I hope you find what you're looking for, Mr Montague,' she called after him as he left the building.

On the way home, he rang his mother. Ten minutes later, she called him back with the information he had asked for. Mrs Clyde had told her that the emergency response team had got Marcel's heart beating again on the way to hospital.

'At what point, though?' Montague demanded.

'There's no need for that tone of voice, David,' she replied. 'Mrs Clyde said they got a pulse as they were pulling into A&E.'

SIX

The Crossing

It had now been several weeks since Elizabeth had visited the house. Back in school, her English class was studying Dickens, and she was intrigued to learn that one of the characters from *Little Dorrit* took a river ferry, similar to the one near where she lived, when he embarked on his journey to visit Mr Meagles at his country residence.

Her teacher, Mr Pankhurst (or 'Peter Pan', as they called him), was delighted when she brought this to the attention of the class. The teacher looked younger than he was and slightly dishevelled. Uncombed hair sat on the collar of a well-worn tweed jacket, paired with cords and deck shoes. He rarely shaved and would survey his students through a pair of old, round, steel-rimmed spectacles. He told them that tomorrow's lesson would take place at the river in the same spot from which their local boat service had been ferrying passengers for nearly four hundred years.

When the class arrived at the river, the teacher told them to gather round. 'This hut marks the spot where the ferry took passengers from the town over to the village on the other side of the river,' he explained. 'It was first established in 1652 by the local earl who owned the stately home over there,' he said, pointing in the direction of the far bank. 'Over 250 years later, in 1909, a local family started up a rival service and charged passengers the princely sum of one penny to cross. Unsurprisingly, the earl's family was furious and wouldn't allow the new service to use the same crossing; so, if you follow me, I'll show you where it still operates to this day.'

Elizabeth was confused. *Where it now operates?* She turned to Freddie Evans, one of the boys in the class. 'The ferry still goes from here,' she whispered. 'I saw it on Friday.'

'Mr Pankhurst?'

'What is it, Freddie?'

'Elizabeth says she saw the ferry here on Friday.'

'What are you doing, Freddie?' Elizabeth hissed. 'I said that to *you*. It wasn't meant for everyone.' She looked at the line of faces now facing her.

Mr Pankhurst smiled. 'That's not possible, Elizabeth,' he said. 'The old ferry stopped running from here seventy-five years ago.'

Rubbish, she thought. Except she thought it a little too hard and the word escaped her lips.

'Elizabeth? What was that?'

'I'm sorry, Mr Pankhurst. I didn't mean—'

'What *did* you mean, then?' he snapped.

Her mind raced. Pan had done his research and would make her look stupid if she tried to argue. 'The ferry may have moved but I saw it here last week,' she replied.

'Perhaps,' he began, 'the tide was strong on Friday, forcing the ferryman to head further upstream in order to reach his destination across the river.'

She nodded and said nothing more.

As the children followed the teacher along the footpath, Elizabeth fell to the back of the group. She had been humiliated and was now confused about what she had seen that night. The point where the ferryman took them across the river was precisely where they had all been standing. She recognised his old shelter, although in the light of day she saw how dilapidated it looked. Pan's suggestion seemed the only explanation.

It was then that she sensed someone behind her and turned to look. 'Tobias! What are you doing here?' It was the first time she had seen him since they had escaped the house together.

'I thought you looked sad.'

In the bright daylight, she realised how slight he was. 'Well, you don't look too good yourself,' she laughed, turning to check on her classmates, who had followed the bend in the path and were now out of sight. 'Our teacher is taking us to where he thinks the ferry crosses the river,' she said. 'I told them I saw the ferryman over there and was made to look a fool in front of the whole class.'

The boy hung his head.

'It's OK, Tobias. It wasn't that bad,' she added.

He stepped towards her. 'Don't tell anyone what you saw. You shouldn't talk about the ferryman – or me, for that matter.'

'Why not?'

'No one must know about the night crossings. They are a secret. Only those invited to the house know about them.'

She looked across to the old ferryman's hut. It was November and already the light had started to go from the day. 'So that's why the ferryman took us from over there: so no one would see. Why did they chase us from the house, Tobias?'

'Because we ran away.'

She grinned. 'That was your idea!'

He smiled and shrugged. 'We don't get many new faces over there and they wanted you for themselves. But I didn't feel like listening to any more conversations from grown-ups,' he explained.

She was about to ask another question when she heard her name being called. It was Pankhurst. He must have noticed that she was missing and come to look for her. She glanced over to where she had last seen them and saw him waving his arms. 'Tobias,' she giggled, 'I'd better go…'

She didn't finish the sentence. He had gone.

'Psst.' It came from the ferryman's hut. She saw movement and the boy crouching in the shadows with his finger to his lips. He smiled and ushered her away with his hand.

'Who were you talking to?'

She was startled. 'Oh, Mr Pankhurst. No one, why?' She panicked, annoyed with herself for inviting another question.

'Miss Fairchild,' he began. 'Firstly, you describe my teaching about the ferry as "rubbish" in front of the other children. Then you break the school's cardinal rule of field trips by separating yourself from the rest of the group. Not only that, but you do it by the river, which is incredibly irresponsible and dangerous.'

She knew he was working himself up for the finale.

'And now you lie to me by saying you weren't talking to anyone when I clearly heard you. This isn't the sort of behaviour I'm used to from you, Elizabeth, so I'd like to know what is going on. Now!' His voice broke as he barked his final demand.

The teacher also taught drama, so she had expected a performance, but was surprised to discover that, like her, he was actually feeling humiliated.

'I'm sorry, Mr Pankhurst, you're right. I got left behind because I was still trying to work out how I could have confused where I saw the ferry crossing. I was talking it through with myself when you came to find me.'

He shook his head, relieved to have found a resolution. 'All right, come on,' he sighed. 'We'd better catch up with the others before we lose them too.'

The boy watched them walk up the path. The others would be angry if they knew that Elizabeth had been talking. He would have to watch her more closely to make sure she didn't betray them. With no one left on the path, the only sound was the river rushing and slopping past his hiding place. A pair of ducks flew fast and low over the trees on the far bank, changing course at the last minute and climbing into the cold, clean expanse above them. Their trajectory set them on a course for the pale moon that was starting to emerge.

That night, Tobias called on her again and she went with him. They were midway across the river when the mist came down. It was imperceptible at first, but then she noticed that the far bank was getting harder to see despite the moonlight. Within moments, they were suspended in a dense cloud of fog. With nothing to see, her hearing became more acute and she listened to the glug and slap of the water against the boat.

'I'm frightened, Tobias.'

He looked across the water. 'Mann, there's something coming,' he said to the ferryman, who lifted his oars out of the water and turned to look.

'You're imagining things. You're as scared as the girl,' he replied.

They started to bob in the water as small waves broke across the bow of the rowing boat.

'Tobias is right!' Elizabeth shouted. A large shape emerged upstream through the gloom and moved silently towards them. 'What is it?' she asked. 'Shouldn't a boat have its lights on at night?'

The ferryman thrust his oars back into the water.

'It's them, isn't it?' Tobias whispered.

'Who, Tobias?' she asked.

'Be quiet, boy,' the ferryman snapped as he pulled on the oars. The craft leapt slightly with each stroke, causing them to bump around on the bench and grab the sides for balance.

The current ran hard now, pushing them off course and making Elizabeth feel nauseous as the hull jumped against the surface. The water smelt dirty and looked dangerous as the waves slobbered against the sides of the boat. 'What's that noise?' she asked, panic in her voice.

Lucas Mann shook his head at Tobias.

'I don't know,' the boy replied.

'Tell me! It sounds like crying.'

'He doesn't know,' the ferryman answered. 'No one does. But we need to be out of the water before it reaches us.'

Before she could ask another question, the wake from the larger vessel rebounded off the near shore and hit the side of their boat, lifting it out of the water. She screamed and fell back, striking her head on the seat and losing consciousness.

When she awoke, the fog had lifted and she found herself gazing at the moon that was now directly above her. She was still in the boat, which had half-lodged itself on the riverbank as the ferryman pulled on the stern to lift it free of the current. She saw Tobias on the bank, looking back at the river. Seeing their lack of concern, she started to cry.

'Looks like your friend's awake. Take her quickly,' the ferryman instructed.

Elizabeth looked at Tobias, who remained staring across the water. 'Is it still there?' she sobbed.

He shook his head. 'We should go in case they come back,' he said.

She eased herself gently out of the boat and clambered up the bank, feeling dizzy. Once they had put some distance between them and the ferryman, she spoke to him again.

'Who are they, Tobias?'

'We don't know,' he said, 'but we are told never to be in the water when they come.'

'Why not?'

When he didn't reply, she tried a different question.

'How often do they come?'

'Sometimes when the moon is full.'

'But why do they want you, Tobias?'

'They don't want me, Elizabeth,' he said.

*

The seasons had begun to change since she'd first visited the woods. The green canopy that had protected them from the elements was gone and leaves floated to the ground like large, rusty snowflakes, pouring out of the sky, dancing, spinning and pirouetting before lying still on the ground. As they made their way through the trees, Elizabeth could hear the soft kissing sound of the leaves dropping around them. She had the sense that time was running out. It made her think of the last grains of sand in an egg timer accelerating away from their glass prison.

'Why didn't you come and see me before?' she said.

Tobias shook his head. 'I couldn't get away.'

'I went down to the ferryman's hut to look for you,' she told him.

They continued walking and she started to kick the dead leaves into the air.

'What do you believe in, Elizabeth?'

She stopped. It was a hard question and she wasn't used to him asking her anything. The boy kept going and she hurried after him.

'I believe in magic,' she giggled.

'I'm being serious,' he said.

'How do you know I'm not?' she asked.

He didn't look at her, so she decided he wasn't impressed with her answer.

'I believe in being kind, wherever possible, and treating others how you would like to be treated.'

'Yes, I've heard that one before,' he replied. 'But why is it important?'

She laughed. This time, he stopped and looked at her, and she saw that he wasn't joking.

'Because everyone wants to be happy, Tobias, and you spread happiness by being kind.'

'What if your happiness comes at the cost of someone else's?'

A dark brown leaf the size of her hand left its home on one of the highest branches and helicoptered its way to the ground, its rotations matching the energy of her thoughts. 'Being kind is more important than your own happiness,' she said.

'Do you really believe that?'

'I think so.' She thought for a moment. 'Because if everyone behaves that way, then no one gets forgotten. And when you're kind it makes you happy too.' She finished with a smile.

Continuing through the woods, Elizabeth was surprised by the size of the trees. They reached up like giant stone pillars supporting a vast brown temple of entwined branches. She hadn't noticed them before and was struck by those lining the path. Stopping to look up, she couldn't even see the tops of several of them. 'Don't you find the trees menacing?' she asked, stopping in front of an ancient oak. It had cracked up the middle, with what looked like an archway carved into its squat trunk.

'What do you mean?'

'They look so angry and... I don't know... fat!' she replied, laughing.

'They're just old.'

She walked towards the tree and gripped the bark. 'Shall we?' It was hard and rough against her hand. She went to step inside, when a noise made her jump.

'They make good nests,' the boy said, laughing.

She ran back to him and watched for movement. When they heard nothing else, they continued on the path.

'What do you think was in there?'

'An animal, I suppose.'

'You don't say, Tobias.'

They walked a little further before she tried again.

'What sort of animal?'

'Probably a fox or a badger.'

'Don't they live underground?'

'Not in here.'

'Why not?'

'They don't need to,' he said.

By now, she hadn't eaten for several hours and was hungry.

'What are you doing?'

'Do you want one? They look lovely.' She smiled, reaching for a blackberry partially hidden by a green leaf.

'Stop!' He ran over as she plucked a plump black fruit from the thorns.

'What's the matter?' she laughed. 'It's only a blackberry. I guess they're late this year.'

'Hasn't anyone told you, "Never eat something you find in a wood"? And anyway,' he paused, 'not everything here is as it seems.' He dropped his head. 'There are things I should tell you.'

Before he could say any more, there was the sound of a tree branch flicking back into position to the right of the path. They wheeled around. Fifty yards away, the outline of a man in a monk's habit dropped to the ground. As he moved towards them, his head was perfectly still.

'Tobias,' Elizabeth cried, 'who is that?'

'Never mind, just run.'

Her lungs burned and she felt light-headed as they took off through the undergrowth. When they passed a squat, bushy tree in a clearing, Tobias stopped running and turned to face her. In the short time she had known him, he had shown little emotion. This time, she saw panic in his eyes.

'We should be safe now.'

She was breathing too hard to speak and fell into a heap on the ground. Her hair stuck to her forehead and beads of sweat rolled over her eyebrows into her eyes. As she waited to catch her breath, she checked that the man wasn't upon them. 'Are you sure he won't find us?'

'He never comes this close to the house.'

Looking ahead, she could make out a faint glow through the trees. 'Who is he?' she asked as they got up and began walking again.

'An outcast,' he replied. 'He crossed my uncle and isn't welcome here any more.'

'What did he want with us?'

The boy looked at her but didn't answer.

'Tobias?'

'He didn't want *us*. He wanted *you*.'

As they continued through the woods, her breathing became laboured and a tear fell from an eyelash and burst on a frosted twig at the side of the path.

'What's the matter?'

'You said a man was after me! I've never seen him before in my life. What does he want with me?'

'The same thing they all want,' Tobias replied. 'They think you can save them.'

'Save them from what?'

'Themselves.'

'I don't understand what that means,' she said.

'Do you remember the book that was missing from the library – the one Solomon brought into the room to show everyone?' Tobias said. 'It is very old. The people in the house believe it has special powers and can tell the future.'

'What's that got to do with me?' she asked.

'The book talks of a time of great happiness. A time free from worry and pain and suffering.'

She shook her head. 'Happiness lives in each of us. It doesn't depend on what a book says,' she replied, suddenly feeling very alone.

'You didn't let me finish,' he said. 'The book tells of one who will come and bring such joy that the greatest party on earth will come to an end and the finest orchestra lay down its instruments.'

'For someone who doesn't say much, Tobias, you're pretty bad at getting to the point,' she replied. 'So who is this person, then? Does the book actually tell you that?'

'Yes, it does,' the boy replied. 'It's you, Elizabeth.'

The next morning, when Elizabeth hadn't come down for breakfast, Mary went to check on her. 'Elizabeth, are you awake?' She knocked gently on the door before opening it. 'Darling?'

Elizabeth kept her head under the covers and groaned.

'Are you all right, sweetie?'

'I've got a headache,' she replied.

'Let me look at you,' her mother said, pulling back the covers. She gasped when she saw the angry bruise on Elizabeth's temple from when she'd fallen in the boat. 'What happened? Did you fall out of bed?'

Tom appeared in the doorway. 'Is everything OK?' He too saw the mark on Elizabeth's face. 'Did somebody at school do this?'

She put her hand to her face and shook her head. 'I fell out of bed,' she said, looking at her mother.

'Maybe we should take you to the doctor this morning to get it checked out,' Mary suggested.

Tom went over and moved Elizabeth's hair away from her face. He looked closely at her eyes to see if the pupils were dilated. 'I don't think she's got concussion,' he said. 'Whereabouts did you bang your head?'

She pointed to the bruise and they all laughed.

'I meant whereabouts on the floor,' he said, still smiling.

'Just there, I guess,' she said.

'You guess?' He pressed the soft carpet with his hand. 'Maybe you caught it on the edge of the bed.'

'Does it really matter, Tom?' Mary asked, stroking the girl's face.

'Well, I'd like to make sure it doesn't happen again,' he said, putting his hands on his hips. 'And it's not going to look very good at school today, is it?' he added, looking at Elizabeth.

Mary suggested that they leave her to get dressed. When they were out of the room, Elizabeth put her hand to her face and winced. Her adventures with Tobias were starting to get dangerous. They were also too exciting for her to stop. When she stood up, a sharp pain in the back of her eye made her blink. It receded to join the dull ache above her cheekbone. She pulled on her school uniform, then brushed her hair and studied the mark on her face. Unlike her father, she couldn't wait for her school friends to see it. Of course, she'd have to be careful not to tell them how she'd got it. That was her secret, and something between her and the strange boy with the blue eyes.

SEVEN

The Librarian

Many years before, when the leaves had fallen from the trees and the mornings broke with a hard frost across the fields, there was a visitor at the abbey. Edward was no longer a novitiate and was now known as Brother Edmund, on the instruction of the abbot. He was walking through the cloister when they heard someone knocking at the main door. He looked across at Brother Regis, who nodded for him to attend to it. They received few visitors, particularly at night.

When Edmund opened the door, he saw a thin old man trying hard to smile. He introduced himself as Solomon, the librarian from the white house on the other side of the woods. Edmund let him in and took him to the chapter house where they could talk. They had to go slowly as the old man seemed in pain when he walked. He told Edmund that word had reached the village of a book about the mysteries of life that was kept at the monastery. He had come to ask if it was true and if he could look at it. Edmund smiled and told him that there was indeed a book that unlocked the meaning of our existence, and that he was sure that Solomon had already seen it, along with countless thousands, in churches up and down the land. His guest tried to hide his irritation by scratching at his face.

Brother Regis then entered the room and, before Edmund had a chance to speak, Solomon introduced himself and said his piece again. The older monk told him that he had heard talk of this before when he was at the market; however, this was the first time someone had asked him about it directly. He explained that the book had been brought to the monastery by Edmund several years ago. Regis added that it was indeed a most interesting read. It also solved none of life's questions.

'In that case,' Solomon smirked, 'you can have no objection to me borrowing it.'

Regis saw from Edmund's reaction that he was unhappy with the idea and told the librarian that the book now belonged to the monastery and must remain within its walls.

Solomon tried again. 'Surely, then, you would be charitable enough to allow me time to look at it today before I leave?'

Regis took a deep breath before nodding his agreement. He asked Edmund to take their guest to the theological hall. As he walked past, Regis held Edmund's sleeve. 'Stay with him,' he whispered, 'and make sure you escort him off the premises when he's finished.'

When he entered the library, Solomon gasped. The librarian was proud of the books he had assembled at the house, but this collection was astonishing. The room was long and high with a sculpted arched ceiling like a Tuscan church. Along each wall were ten rows of books running to the back of the library fifty yards away. There were desks and chairs dotted around the room, and ladders propped against the shelves to allow the monks access to the top rows.

'There are close to half a million books here in the theological hall,' Edmund told him. 'Each one is documented in the register,' he pointed, 'and there is not a single volume that has not been opened and read by a monk from this abbey.'

The librarian was mesmerised. His mouth hung open and saliva pooled at the corners before stretching slowly to his chin. The sensation broke the spell and he wiped his mouth with the back of his hand. Edmund led him to the nearest desk where the book was often left. Its popularity meant that the monks rarely returned it to the shelf. He pulled back the chair for his guest to sit down and retreated to the far side of the hall. The old man sat down and pawed impatiently at the pages. He ran his finger along the lines, keen to digest the information in front of him. After an hour, Edmund cleared his throat. Either Solomon didn't hear, or chose to ignore him and carried on reading. Edmund closed his own book and approached.

'Sir, I have chores I must fulfil,' he said.

Solomon nodded and waved him away.

'Forgive me if I didn't make myself clear,' Edmund continued. 'Guests must always be accompanied in the monastery, so unfortunately I must now ask you to leave.'

Solomon took a deep breath and forced another smile. 'Of course,' he replied. 'I do hope you will allow me to visit another time and continue reading your book.' His emphasis on Edmund's ownership unsettled him.

Edmund returned the smile but didn't reply, instead escorting his visitor out of the library and back to the entrance hall.

Before leaving, Solomon paused and turned to the young monk. 'Why was the book given to you?'

Edmund shook his head.

Solomon turned and walked out of the monastery. 'Something to ponder, then, don't you think?' he asked.

When Edmund was walking back to his cell, he heard his name called. He stopped and waited for Regis to catch up. His mentor was eager to learn what had taken place and was particularly interested in what the librarian thought of the book. Edmund told him that the old man had passed no comment other than to ask why the book had been given to Edmund.

'That, Edmund, was serendipity,' Regis said. 'The man who found you that afternoon in the fields was passing on the holy flame. He stirred your imagination by showing how your life at that time ran in parallel with that of a higher force. Then he changed your path forever by giving you a book that lit the fire for greater understanding.'

Edmund nodded and continued on to his cell. The actions of the stranger all those years ago had indeed led to him joining the monastery. Even so, he was not convinced entirely by Regis's explanation of the man's motive. The image of passing on a flame appealed. It also made Edmund wonder if, with time, he would be required to do the same. And if he was, then he would need to leave the monastery to do it.

It was cold and dark outside and a heavy frost reflected the faint light of a new moon. Edmund watched from his cell window as the frozen path and crystallised grass slowly appeared. When he stepped outside, the air made him cough. He walked towards a sliver of light on the horizon that would lead him to the church. It was dawn on Christmas Day and the service would begin shortly. Yesterday, they had decorated the walls of the abbey with holly and ivy, and fir branches that the monks had harvested from the trees in the grounds.

Inside, the church smelt of incense and candle wax and the air was filled with the sound of industry. Monks were straightening pews, putting out hymn sheets and prayer books, and sweeping the floor. Edmund approached the altar and bowed. Then he turned and walked back down the aisle to the bell tower and took up his position on one of the ropes. The sound of the bells was crisp and full, and he felt their chimes vibrate in his chest. It was the only day of the year when the villagers came to the church at the monastery, and Edmund hoped his mother and father would be there.

In the end, they were among the last to arrive before the doors closed. Edmund was shocked at how they had aged over the last twelve months. They looked tired as they shuffled across the stone floor before choosing a pew at the back of the church. Edmund's mother smiled when she saw him but his father didn't look up, and Edmund could tell that the old man's vision was failing. He wondered how they were coping on the farm. At the end of the service, he sang morning praise with the rest of the choir as the worshippers left the church. When it was over, he left his place in the stalls and slipped out of the side exit of the church, hurrying round to the other side of the building. His parents weren't there. He ran down the path and through the gate before he heard someone calling after him. He turned to see Regis at the door of the church.

'Edmund, is everything all right? Where are you going?'

Edmund looked back and at last spotted his parents, with several others, walking down the track to the village. 'Please, Brother Regis, I need to see them.'

'Edmund, we must tidy the church before breakfast.'

Edmund ran back up the path to Regis and explained that he wanted to speak to his parents, as it was the first time he had seen them all year and he was concerned for their welfare.

The older monk smiled and brought his hands together. 'Of course, my boy. It is Christmas Day. A son must honour his parents.'

When Edmund caught up with them, they had become separated from the group and his mother was helping her husband with his balance. She put her hand to Edmund's face and kissed him. His father squeezed his arm with both hands when he heard his voice.

'I was hoping you might wait for me outside the church,' Edmund said.

'It is cold and I need to get your father back into the warmth.'

The old man's skin was pale and thin. Edmund remembered strong, tanned hands with thick, scarred fingers from working the land. Now his father's touch was soft and uncertain and his fingers were as smooth as a child's. Edmund held them in his hands.

'Have you not been well, Father?'

'Just a little tired, son. It's been another long year.'

Edmund looked at his mother and saw that she was close to tears. 'I'm sorry I haven't been there to help you.' The words left a trail in the air.

'It is not your responsibility, Edward... Edmund. It never has been. You follow a higher path than ours.' His father paused before adding, 'We couldn't be more proud of you.' The old man's eyes were now red and watery, and Edmund started to blink hard himself.

'It is Christmas Day – what is the matter with us?' His mother was always the voice of reason and the two men laughed.

Edmund hugged his parents and said he would pray for them. It was the last time he saw them.

Interest in Edmund's book had led the monks to organise secret gatherings to discuss its meaning in the chapter house. They invited Edmund so that they could hear again about the man who had given it to him and why he might have done so. Edmund would recount it all again and, in time, his story entwined with the legend of the book. Several of the order wondered if it predated the Old Testament. The abbot had told them that that was blasphemous, and that the book's allegories and prophecies were nothing more than plagiarism and derivations of the Scriptures. He compared Edmund's book to the work of a forger trying to copy a masterpiece. Some of the others, including Regis and Edmund himself, were not so sure. There was an authority and a conviction to the writing that suggested it was more than imitation.

As the years passed, Edmund grew certain that the book he had been given as a child was authentic and important. And he was determined to prove it. When their meetings became more formalised, evolving into a monthly reading group, the monks would decide on an agenda by submitting talking points and ideas to Regis. Edmund's suggestions were never chosen. Then, one week, he grew bold with his proposal.

'The final item for discussion today comes from Edmund,' Regis told them.

The younger man was surprised and didn't know where to begin.

'Well?' said Regis.

Edmund stood up and looked at the monks. 'I'm sorry, Brother Regis, but upon further consideration I would like to withdraw my suggestion.'

Some of the monks began whispering. Regis cleared his throat to get their attention.

'Edmund, you have suggested what I'm sure many here are thinking. So please, go ahead,' he instructed.

Edmund slowly got to his feet. He took his time to gather his thoughts. 'I have read the book since I was a boy and for nearly as long as I have studied the Bible,' he began. 'So it has been a part of my life for many years. It has provoked deep thought and stimulated many ideas.'

The monks looked eager to hear what he would say next.

'All of us in this room,' Edmund said, gesturing at them, 'are here because we share a deep fascination with what the book teaches. So I say this. Either it is the missing chapter from the Good Book – and I know the abbot says it is not – or it is a distant echo from another world and we should destroy it now!'

The cocktail of blasphemy and fear of losing something they treasured was too much for some of the monks, who stood up in protest. Brother Percival kicked back his stool, causing it to crash behind him onto the stone floor.

Regis raised his arms, pleading for calm. 'Brothers, please, be still,' he said. 'Edmund, thank you for your contribution. It is not always easy to speak your mind when you know the reaction it may cause.'

Regis turned to Percival and asked him what was the matter. The old monk's face was puce with rage and he tugged at his long grey beard. He could only stammer and bluster incoherently.

'Brother Percival.' Regis raised both hands and took a deep breath.

The other monk took the cue to breathe himself and began to calm down, picking his stool up off the floor.

Regis continued, 'I have said before that we are in possession of something that is indeed powerful and we have just witnessed a demonstration of that potency.'

The monks looked at each other, then nodded in agreement.

'But it is not the voice of Our Father. We hear that only in the Bible,' Regis said.

Edmund raised his hand, but Regis gestured to indicate that he should wait this time.

'And there is no suggestion in any of the many versions we have here at the abbey of a missing chapter, as Edmund suggests.'

'So how can the words be powerful if they are not Our Lord's, nor Satan's either?' Edmund said, unable to stay silent any longer, causing unrest to break out again, with Percival slamming his fist onto the table.

'All right, Percival,' Regis said, raising his voice. 'Brothers, this behaviour will not do.' He let the words hang in the air. After a lengthy pause, he spoke again. 'One day, Edmund, you may venture outside these monastery walls and discover that the thoughts and words of men can carry great power too. And you should rejoice, not be troubled. For we are all God's children.'

Regis saw confusion on their faces.

'The food that we grow, the water we take from the well, the fire that warms us at night are all given to us by God,' he explained. 'The wonder we feel sheltering under the cedar tree on a summer's day, or watching the hares dancing in the spring mist, are evidence of his hand. Equally so, the guides who help us see that majesty are themselves the tools of Our Father.'

'Amen.'

They all turned to see the abbot.

'Come, brothers – you think I was unaware of these secret nocturnal gatherings?' he asked, walking towards them. 'I am pleased you show such a commitment to learning but,' his face hardened, 'we cannot have division in the order.' He walked over to Regis and picked up the book. 'From now on, this remains in the library. Anyone wishing to read it has to speak to me first. I am concerned,' he added, looking at each of them, 'that it is disrupting the harmony of our monastery and distracting us from our daily worship. Until that balance is restored, I demand temperance.'

He turned and walked out with the book, leaving the monks looking at Regis in shock.

'You heard the abbot. It is probably for the best,' he sighed.

EIGHT

The Caretaker

Maurice Truman had been the school caretaker his entire adult life. He'd taken over from a man who had held the post for forty years and he would reach that milestone himself next month. When he'd first started, Maurice had felt like an outsider at the school, with its fancy uniforms and its privileged ways. Down the years, he had softened and now he regarded it as his family; particularly the generations of pupils who referred to him affectionately as 'Mo'.

Despite their familiarity and warmth towards him, Maurice was prone to a deep loneliness that followed him like a shadow, inching closer as each term drew to a close. He was a slight man, and as the weight of the world slowly pushed down upon him, his shoulders began to turn in and his back stooped so that he was barely taller than even the youngest members of the school. The place was now closed for the holidays and he took himself down to the banks of the river. There, he thought about another generation of children who were about to embark on a life outside of the school's four walls. He imagined what lay ahead for them in life. University for most, travelling for others, before inevitably moving on to good jobs in London and other places, where they would raise families of their own. This idea, and that of never seeing them again, was like a nail of sorrow being slowly tapped into his heart, millimetre by millimetre, year after year. He looked out across the river and followed a piece of driftwood. It seemed to have a life of its own, navigating the centre of the river and pushing out ripples ahead of its bow. He wondered how many more summer terms he would see before he too left the school, either through retirement or if they decided it was finally time for a change. Bending down, he picked up a small, flat stone and threw it at the driftwood. Instead of finding its target, the stone took off out of the water, catapulting into the air after kissing the surface. He smiled, remembering how his father had shown him how to skim stones at the seaside.

He did try and think of something purposeful to do with his time during the holidays. But whatever he chose would be a solitary exercise and he was weary of his own company. He looked again at the water and wished it could wash away his troubles and cleanse his soul. The caretaker stood up and shuffled over to the edge of the bank. A small whirlpool appeared a few feet away as the current urged the river towards the next lock and eventually out to sea. The river reflected the moonlight and Maurice imagined being pulled down by its force, spinning round in concentric circles until he reappeared, like Alice through the looking glass, in a world of impossibly vibrant characters who would entertain him and keep him company. He imagined seeing his mother and brother again. Perhaps their father, too, and the family would be complete again.

The motion of the water seemed to draw him closer to the edge, until the spell was broken by unexpected movement. Maurice jumped and turned to see what it was. He froze, continuing to survey the scene for signs of life.

'Hello? Who's there?' He was surprised by how weak and timid his voice sounded. He cleared his throat. 'Come out; I know someone's there,' he demanded, bolder this time. He waited for a reply or another sign of life before letting his breath go in a relieved sigh.

'You sound tired, brother.' The voice was strong and deep and made the hair on the back of Maurice's neck stand on end. The shape of a man emerged from the shed. He was heavyset, with the broad shoulders of a labourer.

'Who are you?' Maurice asked.

'A friend,' the man replied, moving closer.

Maurice made out a wide, dark face with a flat, broken nose and small eyes, and took a step backwards.

'Are you tired?' the man asked. 'Sit here with me on the bank.'

Maurice was surprised to find himself doing as he was told. As his feet hung above the current, the edge of the bank felt soft and comforting on the backs of his knees. 'What do you want?' the caretaker asked.

His new companion stared out at the river. 'None of us meet by chance,' he replied. 'I sensed a soul in need. I've come to help you.'

'You don't look much like a good Samaritan,' Maurice muttered.

The stranger leant towards him. 'I was like you once,' he replied, spitting into the water. Maurice watched it arc from his mouth before vanishing into the surge downstream.

'But the river gave me solace and comfort and has been my companion ever since.'

'I find it soothing,' Maurice admitted, listening to the sound of the water, 'but it's no friend. It hears me but never replies.'

The man stood up. 'What answers are you expecting?'

'This is stupid,' Maurice said, more to himself. 'A river can't solve my problems.'

'Then why do you talk to it?'

Maurice looked at the man, then back at the water as it continued on its relentless journey.

'It answered me and gave me purpose,' the man continued.

'How so?'

'I am the ferryman. The river brings change and new life. It is always moving, yet constant. I can rely on it.'

'And how can that help me? I am a school caretaker. My life is spent cleaning up after children, then waiting for them to return from their holidays.'

The ferryman smiled. 'Then you have time on your hands. And I have more work than one man can handle. Start now and help me tonight.'

He told Maurice about the night service he ran. For the first time he could remember, Maurice Truman acted impulsively and said he would help.

A puff of cloud rushed across the sky and swept over the face of the moon, leaving the shadow of a rainbow in the white cotton-wool vapour.

*

After the abbot had taken the book and the monks had left the room, Edmund stayed behind with Regis.

'Years ago, you were given the book for a reason,' Regis told him. 'The man who gave it to you could have picked anyone. He did not. He chose a child. And his choice was wise. For that child has grown into a man of God who brought the book before a critical audience. But I don't think that is all, Edmund,' he said, placing his hands on the younger monk's shoulders. 'I believe your story will play out in these pages.'

'I don't understand,' Edmund said.

Regis motioned for him to take a seat by the fire. He picked up an iron poker and prodded the logs, causing tiny, glowing particles to fall off the embers and disappear up the chimney. They crackled as they went and Edmund smelt the smoke from the wood as some of it escaped into the room.

'There will come a day, Edmund, when you are called upon to leave this place and continue your journey in the outside world. Your destiny is entwined with the book. It has led you here and one day it will take you away from us.'

'But I'm not ready to leave, Brother Regis. My home is here, in the house of Our Lord.'

'No, Edmund, your home is where the Lord takes you. One day we will look back and see with great clarity the path he has laid out for you.' Regis stood up and moved closer to the fire. He turned his palms to the flames, then rubbed them together. 'I believe the book serves as a map. Your challenge is to learn how to read it. It goes without saying,' he added, 'that I do not share the view of the abbot that the book is counterfeit or without value. Its provenance points to divine origin, as does its teaching.'

'Then—'

'Let me finish, Edmund,' Regis instructed. 'I have searched deep in my heart and cannot shake the conviction that it is somehow linked with Revelation. All of the books saw different iterations before arriving in their current forms. Revelation is no different.'

'You think it could be an early version?'

Regis nodded.

'Why didn't you say so before?!' Edmund asked.

'I needed time to think. Secretly, I hoped you all would arrive at a similar conclusion. Now that forum has been taken from us, my opinion has hardened.'

Edmund was silent and sat with his head in his hands.

'Edmund?'

'I'm sorry, Brother Regis, but this is not what I expected to hear.'

'Yet you thought the same, am I right?'

'No, no, I hadn't quite got that far,' Edmund admitted, smiling. 'Since I was a boy, I believed it echoed the words of Our Lord, but what you're suggesting has enormous implications.'

'The central prophecy?'

Edmund nodded.

'Here's what I know, Edmund. The Bible is the book of man. The Virgin Mary, Mary Magdalene, Martha of Bethany, and any of the other women you may care to mention are described in terms of their relationship to either men or Christ himself. And I think your book tells us something very different. Something that would be considered sacrilege.'

Edmund whispered, 'That a girl could be a messenger of God?'

The older man sighed and looked into the fire as if searching for confirmation. Edmund watched the reflection of the dying flames in his eyes.

'What does the Book of Revelation teach us?' Regis asked.

Edmund smiled as he answered such an easy question. 'At the end of days, the Lord will come again to rid the world of evil and save his children.'

'And how is he described?'

'Surrounded by seven candlesticks and holding a sword.'

'What colour are the candlesticks?'

'Gold.'

'And his clothes?'

Edmund shook his head.

'Edmund?'

'He wears a golden belt.' The younger monk stood up. 'But you can't be suggesting…'

'You must find the golden girl,' Regis instructed.

The two monks were inches apart when Regis spoke again.

'The girl is not a messenger, Edmund. She is Christ.'

On Wednesday morning, Edmund rose early in preparation for visiting the market. The monks were taking honey from the hives and putting it in jars. Edmund helped them, then joined a group from the allotment harvesting fruit and vegetables and stacking them in a wooden trailer. When it was done, they pushed the trailer up the hill towards the monastery. Drawing level with the theological hall, he saw that the door was open. It was unusual for anyone to be in there this early and the order would always close the door behind them. When he looked inside, he knew something was wrong. Books were scattered across the floor and the lectern was on its side, broken. He ran over to the bookcase directly opposite the front door and looked up to the seventh shelf. Fourteen books in from the end of the bookcase, there was a gap. Edmund's book had gone.

Before the trading party left for the village, Regis called everyone together and asked Edmund to break the news. Percival said he had read the book the previous evening and admitted leaving it on the lectern rather than returning it to its place on the shelf. When no one else staked a later claim, Regis declared that a crime had been committed and that there had been an intruder at the monastery. It was the first time it had happened in Edmund's time there and he was certain who was responsible. Several of the others agreed. Regis said it was wrong to jump to conclusions and reminded them to be more charitable. But when he saw that they were all of the same mind, he said he would go to the white house and call on Solomon himself while the trading party was at the market.

In the village that morning, their produce went quickly and they stocked up on rabbits, pigeons and firewood. Returning home, all they spoke of was the theft. The consensus was that Solomon had taken it, either through greed or at his master's bidding, to grace his own library. Word had spread locally about the book at the abbey, but only one outsider had actually seen or read it.

After unpacking the produce from the market, the monks joined the rest of the order for prayers followed by lunch. Regis still hadn't returned, and his delay only added to the intrigue and their excitement to find out what he had learned. By evening prayers, they were getting anxious, and one of the monks suggested sending out a search party. Edmund and some of the others thought it premature and said that their friend had most likely stayed for dinner as a guest at the house.

Solomon Mandrake always carried a book and from the moment he was old enough his greatest joy was to be left in peace in a library. And now he worked in one. He had been at the house for all of his adult life, and had spent the years reading and chronicling the thousands of books in the family's collection. If he had to choose between losing one of his books and losing a member of the household, paper would trump the flesh. People didn't interest him; instead, he preferred the company of books that could transport his mind to more stimulating worlds. What he did enjoy, though, was outsmarting those who got in his way.

Solomon took pride in knowing the whereabouts of every major work and had devoted his life to building a library that rivalled those owned privately anywhere in the country. There were handwritten manuscripts dating back hundreds of years, journals kept by some of the early adventurers, alongside works by some of the great academic minds. There were books on navigation and geography, physics and geometry, chemistry and biology, philosophy and psychology. Yellowed parchment pages bound between thin wooden boards told tales of unchartered seas and hell-sent sea monsters, written in the floral hand of the explorers.

The biggest section in the house's library was reserved for religion. All the major beliefs and philosophies were represented, from Christianity and Islam to Hinduism and

Sikhism through to Judaism and Buddhism. And yet there was one book the librarian treasured above all others. His latest acquisition. It was wide and heavy, making it impossible to pick up with just one hand. The book had a thick leather cover that was ribbed every few inches for added strength, and its brown sleeve had faded to yellow from the corrosive combination of sunlight and sweaty fingers. No one, not even Solomon, knew who had written it. He did know, of course, where it came from. And, unfortunately, the book was simply too valuable to return to the monastery.

He had discovered its existence quite by chance when talking to the villagers at the market. At first, the monks were suspicious and made sure that someone was always with him in the octagonal room where the book was kept. As his visits became more frequent, they left him alone to read. It was then that they let down their guard. He overheard three of them come in and say that they would discuss the idea that the book could be the missing testament that very evening. When they arrived at the section of the library where the book was kept and saw Solomon reading it, they stopped talking immediately and looked at one another.

'Don't mind me, gentlemen, just finishing up here,' he remarked, slamming it shut with delight and grinning at them. 'It really is so very fascinating, don't you think?' he asked, walking past them.

They didn't reply and Solomon decided that he would come back to the monastery just one more time. That was all he needed.

He could already recite several sections of the book with his eyes closed. One passage in particular gave Solomon the most pleasure. Its words fell into place with perfect synchronicity and played on the ear like the sweetest melody.

The earth is full of wonder,
But heaven awaits the true.
To cross the great divide,
A child must believe in you.

The old man sighed with satisfaction and brought his hand to his chest. He turned at the sound of laughter.

'I've told you before, Solomon, not to get yourself so excited.' The duke was smiling, although his eyes were serious.

'It's here in front of us,' Solomon replied. 'This is what we have waited all these years for.'

Charles Featherstone raised his hand to silence him. He walked to the lectern, forcing Solomon to stand aside, and read the page. 'My family has kept you under this roof since before I was born because they were of the understanding that you had a brilliant mind,' he explained. 'At your disposal is a library that is the envy of some of the world's greatest seats of learning, yet the best you can come up with are these nursery rhymes from a book you stole from a monastery!' He stamped his foot in anger and a light veil of dust lifted above his shoe and danced in the light. 'In case you hadn't noticed, we have a child of our own here who brings me no closer to enlightenment than the rats in the kitchen,' he growled, slamming the book shut.

'How wrong you are,' Solomon said.

'What did you say?' The duke marched towards him until their faces were inches apart.

Solomon swallowed.

Featherstone's voice dropped in pitch. 'I asked you a question, old man.'

Before Solomon could answer, Gabriella entered the room and approached her husband. 'I heard raised voices.' She smiled.

'Our great thinker here has something to tell you,' the duke replied.

Solomon cleared his throat and looked at the duchess. She could be as cold as her husband and yet, to him, her beauty and occasional sensitivity offset it. He repeated his belief that not only was the book the missing scripture; it answered many of the questions raised by the Bible. He added that he'd heard several of the monks say the same, when unaware that he was listening. He leant towards her conspiratorially. 'Its overriding theme is the value of children and their central role in prophecy.'

She put her hand on her husband's shoulder before he could scold the old man again. 'So how does this help us?' she asked Solomon.

He motioned for her to come over. He opened the book and turned page after page, throwing up fine particles into the air as he looked for his spot. 'It's here,' he said, pointing at a page.

She read the section on the lost tribe and the prophecy of the golden girl. 'Have you seen this?' she asked her husband.

'How do we know this isn't a fairy tale?' he demanded.

'I know it from the depths of my soul,' the librarian replied. 'And so do the monks, which is why they guarded it so carefully. They even had secret readings of it.'

Before he could say any more, they heard knocking at the front door.

*

It had been a cold morning when Regis first came to the abbey. Although it was many years ago, he still remembered it clearly. The crunch his footsteps had made on the path to the front door, and the way the air froze the hairs in his nose and made them crackle when he breathed.

He had always wanted to be a monk. After growing up in an orphanage, his life was shaped by the kindness of nuns, and it left a lasting impression of the power of goodness. The sisters were his family and he knew that without them he would not have survived. He could remember nothing of his parents and there was no one else to look after him. The nuns' actions showed him the meaning of love, faith and charity. It was hope he found most redemptive. Regis believed that without hope, life was insufferable. However terrible things seem, if you have reason for hope, then there is a sliver of light to lead out of the darkness. He was living proof of it.

As he made his way to the white house, the overnight frost lingered on the fields and made him think again of that morning all those years ago. He had been sure that it was his destiny, although at the time he was still nervous about what awaited him inside and if the other monks would like him. He sighed now when he realised that a young man's feelings of trepidation had never left him. He was approaching the later years of his life yet he was still unsettled by the idea of unfamiliar social interaction.

That, probably, was to be expected. However carefully he broached the subject, he was going to have to ask Solomon if he had taken the book. It was a serious accusation and unlikely to be received well.

As Regis neared the house, part of him hoped that he would find no one home and could go back to the monastery to see if others had news. Deep down, he knew he was at the right place and that such a large house would always have someone to answer the door. He took a deep breath to settle his nerves and brought the knocker down on its metal plate. He counted to ten, relieved not to hear movement inside. He would try knocking one more time and if there was still no answer, he could assume no one was home. When he lifted the knocker for a second time, it came out of his hand as the door was opened from the inside.

The gardener had watched the bald, squat monk approach the house. It was unusual for visitors to come to the house during the day and he noticed how the man slowed the nearer he got. The monk stopped when he was twenty yards away from the front door and looked around to see if anyone was there. The labourer stayed out of sight in the woodshed.

The visitor approached the house. The gardener smiled at the futility of his journey. *If he's come here thinking they'll make any donations to the monastery, then he's more stupid than he looks.* He chuckled. When the door opened, he recognised the angular form of Solomon. The monk did most of the talking, before the librarian looked past him to see if anyone was watching and then beckoned his visitor inside. The gardener lifted the wicker basket containing the logs and made his way to the side of the house. After taking them into the boot room, he returned for another load, struggling a little more under the weight.

When he got back to the house, he heard shouting. It stopped the moment he dropped the basket on the floor. He cursed himself and decided to keep quiet in the hope that the quarrel would continue. Before long, he heard Solomon in the next room, talking in angry whispers, while his guest maintained a calm tone. He had obviously said something to enrage the librarian again, who responded by calling him a mistaken fool. The gardener decided that the visit was unlikely to be about a charitable donation and pressed his face against the door. As gently as he could, he turned the handle and pushed it open a fraction. The monk was facing Solomon, who had his back to the gardener. All three then heard footsteps on the stairs. From where he crouched, the gardener couldn't see who it was. He watched both men turn to face the newcomer.

'Solomon, what is all this noise?' asked the duchess. 'And why didn't you tell me we were expecting a visitor?' She continued down the stairs and offered the monk her hand.

The librarian said that Brother Regis had made a mistake and had come to the house to look for a book taken from the monastery. The monk's face flushed and he tried to soften the accusation.

'Solomon, I thought you had it?' the duchess asked.

Regis stopped talking. His eyes darted from Gabriella to Solomon and back again. The librarian said nothing and looked at the duchess, who was smiling.

'Solomon, why don't you go and get my husband so we can discuss this? What do you say, Brother…?'

'Regis,' the monk replied.

'Regis, yes, that's it,' she repeated. 'What a grand name for such an unremarkable-looking creature,' she laughed. 'Of course we must reunite you with your missing book.'

After the gardener quietly pulled the door shut, the duchess called his name. He left his hiding place and entered the drawing room, removing his cap and holding it against his leg.

'I thought I told you we wanted a fire.'

'I was just collecting the wood, ma'am.'

'Send someone in here to light it immediately.'

The gardener tipped his head and backed out of the room.

'I must apologise for the temperature in here, Regis. It's enough to chill your soul, don't you think?' she asked.

He replied that it was really not too bad and that he had dressed appropriately for such a cold day.

After the fire was lit, Solomon returned with the duke.

'There you are, darling!' the duchess exclaimed. 'May I introduce Brother Regis?'

The monk stood up. The duke ignored his hand.

'It seems Solomon here borrowed a book from our friends at the abbey and – how shall I put it? – forgot to return it.' She raised her eyebrows.

The duke glared at Solomon. Regis was struck by the piercing green colour of his eyes and the intensity of his gaze.

'I'm sure it's all just a small misunderstanding,' Regis said, attempting a smile. 'At the monastery, we have been most impressed with Mr Mandrake's dedication to study and, of course, his regular visits to see us.'

'I didn't come to see *you*,' Solomon snapped.

'You idiot,' the duke said to him. 'You have brought this upon us.'

The duchess stood up. 'Solomon, why don't you take Regis to find his book?' she said.

The librarian looked at the duke, who nodded.

'I'll take you to the library,' Solomon said to Regis, following him out of the room.

When they had gone, the duke went into the storeroom where the gardener had left the baskets of wood with his axe. Then he, too, headed for the library.

NINE

—

Wolf Moon

Elizabeth had lived all of her life in the same house. She was drawn to the river beyond her garden because it was governed by the moon, which she had loved from the moment she had first seen it as a small child. Tonight, when she observed it from the kitchen, it seemed as fresh as the rising sun, perfectly formed and illuminating the silver clouds that passed beneath. She knew that the full moon in January was a Wolf Moon and she gave an involuntary shiver, imagining a howling silhouette against the brilliant white backdrop. She felt a hand on her shoulder and jumped.

'Jesus Christ! Whatever's the matter, Elizabeth? You nearly gave me a heart attack.'

'Gave *you* a heart attack?!' Her eyes widened. 'How about not creeping up on people like that?'

Tom held up his hands. 'I didn't know you were so jumpy.'

Before she could answer, Mary came in. 'Everything OK?'

Elizabeth looked at her father and frowned.

Mary smiled and said, 'Look at the full moon,' pointing over their heads.

Elizabeth didn't want to share the moment with them and looked away. She felt an urge to throw open the back doors and step outside. Instead, she decided to wait until they had gone to bed.

Later that night, when her bedside clock showed it was midnight, she slipped out from under the duvet and got dressed. Her feet settled gently on each step going down the stairs as she listened for her parents. In the hall, she took her coat and boots from the cupboard and unlocked the back door. The garden was bathed in a dreamy white light that made the lawn and plants appear as if they had been sketched in chalk. When she was clear of the house, she breathed deeply and looked up to take in the view.

Instead of feeling wonder, her breath caught in her throat and her stomach loosened. Against the lunar backdrop, the shadow of a wolf's head appeared in vivid relief: snarling, fur on end. She turned for the house and started to run. Then, she heard laughter. Spinning around, she looked again at the moon. The outline of the wolf slowly dissolved into the branches of a fir tree.

'Thought you saw something, miss?' The man chuckled before clearing his throat and spitting onto the ground.

The ferryman, she thought. She tiptoed back towards the house.

'Aren't you going to say hello?' he teased. 'The boy misses you.'

Elizabeth stopped. 'Where is he?'

'Waiting with my boat,' the voice called out, sounding further away.

Despite the temperature, she was flushed. She looked

again at the moon and saw only the branches of the tree swaying. She tried to imagine how they could have come together in the shape of a wolf. A flash of light caught her eye and she saw the bathroom light come on upstairs. Would they look out the window and see her out here in the moonlight? She decided it was more likely that she'd be spotted out here than found missing from her room, so her decision was made. Peering through the hedge at the end of the garden to make sure Lucas Mann wasn't there, she ran to the gate, quietly lifting and replacing the metal latch before stepping onto the footpath. She could just make out the figure of the ferryman entering his hut. Then, she saw Tobias coming towards her.

'Isn't it beautiful, Tobias?!' she purred, pointing past him to the river that had barely a ripple on its glassy surface. On the far bank, the trees held their poses like elegant old ballerinas arching tired limbs.

He looked confused.

'Over there,' she explained, 'on the other side of the river.'

'Why do you say that?' he asked.

She laughed. 'Are you serious? The trees and the soft grass in the moonlight. It's like a painting. Come on, let's go and find your friend, the ferryman.'

'He's not my friend,' the boy replied, walking in step with her.

When they reached the hut, Elizabeth's foot caught a small pebble that flew across the path and cannoned off the wooden structure. There was a grunt inside and Lucas Mann poked his head out of the window.

'Decided to come after all, then,' he said.

'Will you take us across?' Elizabeth asked.

'He can't,' Tobias whispered.

'What?' Elizabeth said.

'Ignore the boy,' the ferryman said. 'I will take you across when it's time.'

'But that's silly,' Elizabeth said. 'There's no current at all and we could be over in a minute.'

'Don't, Elizabeth…' Tobias warned her.

He was cut short by the ferryman stepping in front of her. Up close, she could see every line and crack on his face, pockmarked and scarred. The pores on his nose were deep and wide and filled with dirt. Worse was his breath, which smelt like an abattoir on a hot day; its pungent, meaty odour worming its way down her throat and tugging at her guts. She felt the contents of her stomach rising and closed her mouth to stop herself vomiting. When he spoke again, she smelt all that was rotten in the world. A cold sweat crawled over her brow and cheekbones.

'This boat crosses the river when I say so,' he spat. 'When you step on board, you are in my world, of which you know nothing. So do as I say and don't question me again.'

'Leave her alone!' Tobias shouted, standing between them.

The ferryman raised his hand. 'Back, boy, or you'll feel my fist,' he growled.

'You wouldn't dare touch me,' Tobias challenged, staying where he was.

The man snorted and grimaced at Elizabeth. She felt another wave of nausea. He moved his finger to lift a strand of hair away from her face, causing her to flinch and move out of reach.

'Think you're untouchable too, do you?' he asked, turning away and returning to his shelter.

'Don't worry about him,' Tobias said. 'He's like an angry dog on a chain. He may snarl and snap but he can't bite us.'

She kept her eyes on the hut. 'He's a hateful creature, Tobias, and I wish he was on a chain,' she said, her voice trembling. 'Sadly, he's not, and I don't feel safe around him.'

'It's just his way of asserting his authority, of which he has none, by the way,' he added, smirking.

'What did he mean by "untouchable"?' she asked.

Tobias's expression changed. 'If he harmed either one of us, my family would punish him,' he explained. 'The river is all he cares about and they would take it away from him, and he would never risk that.'

'So he works for your family?'

'Kind of,' he said. 'The ferryman is busy right now with our parties and he wouldn't want to lose that custom.'

She didn't reply.

'Was there something else?' he asked.

She went to speak, then stopped.

'Tell me,' Tobias said.

'You said he wouldn't want to lose the trade from the parties.'

'That's right.'

'Well, doesn't trade involve some kind of payment?'

'What do you mean?'

'I've just realised that we've never paid him for the crossings,' she said, 'and he's never asked, although you once said that people do pay him.'

'It will be paid all right.'

They looked round to see that the ferryman was back.

'Particularly for you, miss,' he laughed.

'You idiot – watch your tongue,' Tobias hissed.

Elizabeth tried to change the mood. 'Mr Mann, do you think we could perhaps go across the river now?'

He continued to glare at Tobias, then nodded. 'The tide is good. We'll cross now,' he said.

There was no further conversation as the three of them crossed the river. The wind had picked up and pale-blue cigar-smoke clouds blew across the sky, lit by the watching moon. Elizabeth played out in her mind what had just happened. Tobias was not as timid as he appeared, and the ferryman was undoubtedly a brute who resented him and his family. He also respected their authority. And yet there was something more.

When they reached the bank, she noticed the boy looking at her. When she went to speak, he shook his head and gestured to get out of the boat. After they had crossed the towpath and reached the woods, she tried again.

'Why did you call him an idiot?'

'Because he is. And he's rude.'

'That's not what I meant,' she said. 'You were angry when he said he would be paid for taking me across.'

He ignored her and continued walking. She kept pace with him for a while, then stopped. She watched as he moved further away until he must have sensed that she was no longer with him. She stared at the back of his head and waited for him to answer. It was much colder in the woods and a damp, fine mist made him appear slightly out of focus. She didn't see him turn around to face her.

'I told you he works for my family,' he said, smiling now. 'It has been a long time since I've had a friend at the house and they are pleased.'

'Why are they pleased?' she asked.

He moved towards her and his eyes sparkled with warmth and happiness. 'My aunt says I am a lonely boy. She will be happy to see I have a friend, and the ferryman knows that when my aunt is happy, he will be looked after.'

There was a hollow feeling in Elizabeth's stomach and she could feel her heart thumping in her chest. 'If that's true,' she began, 'then why was he stupid for saying so?'

'Because it's not for him to comment on anything my family does,' Tobias replied. 'He should show more respect and he shouldn't behave towards our guests the way he did to you.'

She looked unconvinced, so he bounded over to her.

'Come on, Elizabeth,' he cajoled. 'We're going to have such fun tonight. Ignore that fool and let's get going.'

She looked into his blue eyes and couldn't help but go with him.

*

The following morning, the monks finished prayers and had a breakfast of oats and water. Before setting out to work in the fields, it was agreed that everyone would help to look for Regis if he hadn't returned by lunch. Their search would centre on the route to the house, as well as the village, in case anyone had spotted him there.

Later that afternoon, when they arrived at the house, Edmund led the group up the drive that was flanked by twin regiments of tall, thin trees. Although he had not been here before, he knew of the place from when he'd lived on the farm, as it was the biggest house in the area. Edmund went up the steps. He knocked on the door with a wooden staff. The rest of the monks stayed back on the driveway. Edmund had expected one of the servants to greet them, so was surprised when the door was opened by the duchess.

'Have you come to save us?' she laughed.

Her remark caught him off guard and he looked back at the others. Brother Percival nodded and waved him on.

'Forgive me, madam. We are looking for our brother, Regis. We were hoping you might have seen him,' Edmund said.

'Should I have?' Gabriella turned her head quizzically to one side.

'He was coming here yesterday morning to visit the librarian,' Edmund explained, 'and he hasn't returned.'

She asked Edmund to come in. He looked past her into the hall and saw family portraits hanging from the walls. She took him into a small reception room with a leather sofa and two chairs. The room was warm and smelt of the fire that still glowed under a white marble mantelpiece. Edmund saw that it had burned all night and the last embers nestled in a soft pillow of grey ash.

'Can I get you something to drink?'

'No, I'm fine, thank you,' Edmund replied. He looked at his feet as he shuffled towards the fire.

'You haven't told me your name.'

Edmund looked up. 'Forgive me, madam – my name is Brother Edmund, from the abbey.'

She giggled. 'I had no idea.'

He blushed and looked away again.

Gabriella smiled and put her hand on his elbow. 'Don't be shy, Edmund, I was just having a little fun,' she said. 'Why don't you sit down and tell me all about Regis?'

He did as he was instructed, and told her about the theft from the abbey and the missing book. As his story progressed, he became uncomfortable articulating their suspicion that Solomon was responsible.

'Edmund, you're not suggesting...'

The young monk felt a bead of perspiration on his forehead and wiped it away quickly with the back of his hand. 'No, no, of course not,' he stammered. 'We simply wanted to see if Solomon might know who else held such an interest in the book that they might take it.'

'And that's why your colleague was coming to see us yesterday?' she asked.

Edmund caught movement out of the corner of his eye. A handsome man with oil-black hair entered the room.

'Have you met my husband, Edmund?'

'I'm sorry, no, sir, I haven't.'

'Edmund here is looking for a friend of his who appears to have got lost,' she explained. 'And he thought dear old Solomon might know where he is.'

Her husband moved his arm from his side and turned a small axe in his hand. 'That's a shame,' he said, as he crouched on the hearth and began splitting kindling. A couple of times, the axe cannoned off the stone plinth and sparks flew into the air.

'Yes,' his wife continued, 'it is a shame, because Edmund and those friends of his waiting outside hoped we might have news of the little lost lamb.'

The duke stopped and stood up, looking out of the window at the other monks. Then he bent down again and continued chopping the wood, harder this time.

'I'm sorry, Edmund,' the duchess apologised, stepping

towards him. 'Solomon is away at the moment so Regis couldn't have met with him.' She then gestured towards the door and walked Edmund back into the hall.

After thanking her for her time and apologising for the intrusion, he left to tell the others what had happened. If Regis hadn't made it to the house, then he must have discovered something closer to home. The search party moved off down the drive while the duchess and her husband watched from the window. Solomon stood behind them.

Regis had still not returned. The monks had retraced the steps of their friend many times and several people had said that they had seen him leave the village in the direction of the house. There was no proof that Solomon, or any of the others, knew what had happened to Regis. Circumstantial evidence indicated that he'd gone missing between the village and the house while going to see the librarian, and that was suspicious. So too was the behaviour of the duchess, who'd showed no concern for his whereabouts.

There was a much shorter route to the house from the abbey. If you left the track before the bend and negotiated the steep bank at the side of the pine copse, the distance was less than half a mile. Once through the trees and over the dyke, you would approach the grounds at the rear of the house. Edmund set off using the half-moon to guide him. It was cold and the grass looked frosted. He knew this was an illusion as the air did not bite his lungs. He was still uneasy after his previous visit and wasn't exactly sure why he needed to return, other than to look for clues and hope to observe any unusual behaviour.

As he navigated through the trees, he thought about how

much his life had changed since leaving the farm. The boy who had left home to join the monastery was now a man and yet his mission was a singular one. Despite immersing himself in monastery life, if he was honest with himself, his studies and his worship had been sidelined by the book. It was what had inspired him to join the order and it retained its spell over him. Kicking through the sedge and long grass that pulled at his shins, Edmund realised that the book had also led him to this point. Regis had left the monastery in the hope of recovering it and now Edmund was doing the same, although he told himself that his primary motive was finding his friend. The thought that he was being manipulated by a book – whose provenance was uncertain – made him uneasy.

When he came to the dyke, there was a dead tree he used as a crossing point. He stretched out his arms for balance and carefully walked across. At the midway point, his foot slipped on the bark and he did a partial pirouette, foot in the air and arms flapping, in a bid to recover his balance. After a moment of panic, he regained his composure and returned his flailing foot to the fallen trunk. His relief at doing so led him to overcompensate by bending too far forward and the added momentum sent him head first into the water. Though shallow, it was deep enough to soak him, and the impact grazed his hands and knees. He pulled himself up on the far bank using nettles that stung his hands. He lay on his back in pain. The shock of the fall had brought home the gravity of the situation and showed him how easily he could be hurt.

'Who are you?'

Startled, Edmund sat up.

'Are you hurt?' It was a boy with remarkably blue eyes.

'I fell in the dyke. I'm all right, though,' Edmund replied.

'What are you doing here?'

'I was trying to find my way back to the monastery and got lost,' Edmund lied, which made him feel guilty. He quickly gave a silent prayer for forgiveness. 'Do you live here?' It was an obvious question and he needed time to think what to do next.

'I live here with my aunt and uncle. My name's Tobias.'

It was late for someone of the boy's age to be awake, let alone outside at this time of night, Edmund thought. 'Shouldn't you be in bed, young man?'

The boy looked back at the house. 'Do you want to come inside and get dry?'

'No, thank you. I should get back now.'

'Do you have a question? You can ask me anything.'

Edmund was surprised, then thought for a moment. 'Does the librarian, Solomon, live with you?'

'Yes. Are you his friend?'

'No. I think he may have borrowed a book from the abbey where I live,' Edmund replied. He was unable to keep eye contact with the boy and looked down.

'Solomon is in the library now. Why don't you come and ask him?'

Edmund remembered the duchess telling him that Solomon was away. Before he could reply, someone called from the house.

'Tobias? Where are you?'

When the boy turned to see, Edmund jumped up and ran for the dyke, deciding this time to vault it. He reached the far bank and managed to haul himself up without getting wet again.

'I'm late and have to go,' he called back. 'Thank you for your help.'

*

Late one evening, after the boy had come to meet Elizabeth and they'd reached the hut, they saw that the ferryman was not alone. Tobias stopped walking.

'What's wrong?' Elizabeth asked.

The boy stared at the two men waiting by the riverbank.

'Tobias?' she said, watching the muscles flex in his jaw.

'The ferryman is meant to work alone,' he replied. 'What we do is private.' He started walking again, this time with purpose.

Suddenly, Elizabeth called out, 'Mo! Is that you?'

The school caretaker raised his hand sheepishly.

'I didn't know you worked on the river too,' she said.

'He's helping me tonight,' the ferryman said.

Tobias glared at him.

Elizabeth thought Maurice looked sad and wondered if he was ill. His cheeks seemed more sunken than usual and his eyes were dull. 'Are you OK, Mo?' she asked.

He gave her a faint smile. 'Yes, of course, Miss Fairchild,' he replied. 'Thank you for asking.'

'Fairchild?'

Elizabeth looked at the ferryman.

'Fair-child,' he repeated, nodding as he said her name. 'Of course, now it makes sense,' he said, looking at Tobias.

'What does?' she asked.

'Just ignore him,' Tobias interrupted, moving towards the small rowing boat moored against the jetty. 'Come on

110

then, caretaker, do your job and help us aboard,' Tobias instructed.

Maurice untied the boat and held it close so they could climb in. When they were ready, the ferryman told him to wait there for them and pushed the boat away from the bank with an oar. Elizabeth shuffled closer to Tobias and asked quietly what the ferryman was talking about.

'He doesn't know who you are and your name has no significance to him,' Tobias replied. 'His job is to ferry people across the river. He thinks he's more important than he is and he likes to pretend he knows what's going on, that's all.'

She wondered what significance her name could have. Equally alarming, she tried to imagine what was going on if they weren't simply going to the party again. She felt nervous and the choppy crossing was making her feel sick. Once they were away from the ferryman, she wanted answers. If Tobias refused, or she was dissatisfied with what he said, she would return to the riverbank. At least with Mo nearby, she had someone she could trust. Despite her anxiety, it was still late and she started to feel very tired. Tonight, there was a large cushion in the stern of the boat, and when she lay back, its soft embrace and the gentle movement of the water rocked her to sleep.

Within moments, the wind picked up and the crossing became choppy. A wave broke across the bow, hitting Tobias in the face, who turned in panic, asking if they would drown. Before the ferryman could answer, Elizabeth spoke. When they looked at her, they saw she was still asleep.

'Don't worry, it's OK,' she said softly. 'Calm down.'

It seemed she was talking to Tobias, but her words could have been uttered to the gathering storm, which died as quickly as it had begun. They looked around in surprise. Elizabeth opened her eyes and asked Tobias what was the matter. He turned to the ferryman, whose mouth hung open. He shook his head at the boy, who told her he had been splashed by a small wave that had made him jump.

*

The third moment that changed Edmund's life came when he found the book again and realised its potential for evil. His encounter with the boy when he'd tried to reach the house had frightened him. Deep down, he knew he must return. He had a feeling that the disappearance of Regis was tied to the book and finding one would lead to the other. Edmund believed Solomon was the key to the mystery and that was cemented when the librarian's visits to the monastery stopped immediately after the book's disappearance. Solomon had either grown tired of studying the book – which was unlikely, as his passion for reading it matched theirs – or he knew it was no longer there.

This time when Edmund returned to the house, he made it through the woods and into the grounds without incident. Before setting off, he had waited until the clock in the abbey had chimed three times to be sure everyone in the house would be asleep, hopefully including the strangely nocturnal boy. He wasn't sure what he'd do when he arrived, so began by looking through the windows to see if anything seemed unusual. The first room he peered into was a drawing room. The fireplace was empty and there were no other signs anyone had been in there recently.

Creeping round the building, he peered into a larger

room with a half-burned log in the grate that smoked gently like a cigar. A noise from inside the house made him jump and he crouched down, pressing himself against the wall. He heard it again and realised it was the sound of a chair, or a table leg, being moved across a wooden floor. He had hoped not to find anyone and now regretted coming back. He waited until it was quiet again and then stayed where he was for another few minutes to be safe. Hoping the danger had passed, he stepped back from the wall and scanned the building, trying to work out where exactly the noise had come from. Looking up to the next floor, there was light from a room in the middle of the house that had a mature climber running up from the ground to its window. Although the plant looked dead, its trunk and branches were thick. Edmund pulled at it: gently at first, and then harder to make sure it held strong on the stone and mortar. He gripped it above head height and began to climb. It was surprisingly easy and made the perfect ladder.

When he reached the window, he tilted his head back to raise his eyes above the sill. The room was full of candles that cast flickering shadows onto the ceiling. He could hear talking but couldn't see anyone. He pulled himself a little higher and looked into the left-hand side of the room. Charles Featherstone sat in an armchair in front of the fire, holding a glass of brandy. On the table next to him was an empty decanter. Edmund couldn't see who he was talking to. Even with his ear against the window, he couldn't make out their conversation. To discover the identity of the other person, he pulled himself up further. As he did, a figure moved past the window, surprising him, and he lost his grip. He fell, catching his foot between the wall and one of the limbs of the vine, halting his descent. He hung upside down, staring at the lawn below. The talking in the room grew louder and he heard someone moving closer to the window. It creaked open and he saw Solomon's crooked nose. The old man squinted to adjust his eyes to the darkness and survey the grounds.

'What is it, Solomon?'

Solomon didn't reply, but continued to look into the darkness. 'There's nothing there,' he said. 'It must have been a fox or some deer.'

He slammed the window and Edmund heard him speak again. His voice grew quieter as he moved further into the room. If he had looked down against the side of the house, he would surely have seen Edmund. The foot he'd trapped was now starting to hurt from his weight pulling down on it. He took a deep breath and sat up quickly, reaching for the vine. He nearly made it, then lost his grip, and his fingernails pulled and split the bark, causing him to fall back again. On the next attempt, he managed to get a hold with one hand and then pull himself closer to grip the vine in both. By taking the pressure off, he was able to inch his foot out of the snare. Returning to a standing position on the climber, he took a moment to catch his breath and think. If he gave up now, he wasn't sure he'd have the courage to return again. He said a prayer and started to climb.

This time when he looked through the window, Solomon was in front of him with his back to the window. He was reading, and Featherstone and his wife, Edmund now saw, were listening. Despite slamming the window, Solomon had failed to put it on the latch and the stiff hinge had forced it open slightly, allowing Edmund to hear what they were saying.

'There can be no other interpretation, Your Grace. The passage is very clear.'

Charles Featherstone waved the arm holding his drink. 'A child?' he snorted. 'What ungodly ideas you have, Librarian.'

'It didn't bother you about the monk, though, did it?' Solomon replied.

Featherstone threw his glass into the fireplace and lurched towards him.

'Charles,' his wife said, grabbing his arm. 'Solomon is wise. Please listen to him.'

Edmund could see the duke breathing heavily through flared nostrils as he tried to calm down. He staggered towards Solomon and said something Edmund couldn't hear. Solomon closed the book and Edmund recognised that it was his. The shock made him wobble on the climber and hold on tighter, looking down and realising for the first time how far he was from the ground. When he looked up again, the window opened hard into his face, catching him on the chin and knocking him off the wall. He braced himself for impact but felt nothing.

*

Edmund woke on the grass. It was a beautiful morning and he saw long streaks of cloud embossed upon the bright-blue backdrop high above him. He was surprised the people in the house hadn't taken him. He listened to the chorus of early-morning birdsong, then slowly got to his feet and looked up at the window. It was a long drop and yet he had no injuries. It was a miracle he'd survived and he thanked the Lord for his mercy.

He thought back to what had happened. Solomon had stolen the book and then tried to kill him. It confirmed what he'd already suspected: that his friend Regis must also have discovered too much. Edmund knew that once Solomon and the others realised that he was still alive, he would be in great danger. He was not the only one. Last night, they'd spoken of a child and a course of action so repugnant even Charles Featherstone had called it ungodly. Edmund didn't need to hear the details to know which passage of the book they had been discussing. What he didn't understand was why they would want to hurt a golden girl.

TEN

Footprints in the Snow

February brought snow for the first time in many years. The north of the country froze every winter, with the chill descending from the mountains onto the villages and towns. It rarely made it as far as London. The capital hummed with an industrious energy that kept the cold at bay. This year was different. The weather usually came from the south-west; instead it moved in from the east this time.

The snow arrived in a bruised black sky that spread silently overhead. It dimmed the light from the day, before releasing millions of dancing, frozen flakes that parachuted to earth. Elizabeth watched them from the kitchen with her nose pressed against the back doors. Her breath steamed the glass, forcing her to rub it with her sleeve. Tom came in and took his phone from his pocket. He brought it to his face and adjusted the focus before taking several photographs of her golden silhouette against the white backdrop.

She heard the clicking of the electronic shutter and turned round. 'Isn't it magical, Daddy?' She smiled, gliding towards him.

He pulled her close and kissed her forehead. They stood together, watching the snow layer the garden and soften the sharp edges of the branches.

Later that day, they fetched their rubber boots and pulled on heavy coats and stepped into the garden. Elizabeth felt each foot sink a couple of inches until her weight compacted the snow and provided a sure footing. It gave way with a satisfying creak as they made their way towards the back gate. When they reached the end of the garden, Tom shook the lower branches of a tree and it reminded her of the snow globe they put on the mantelpiece at Christmas. A cloud of white particles filled the air before dropping to the ground in a heartbeat. They looked out across the towpath to the river. It was silent and the water moved in slow motion. A solitary swan used the current to propel itself downstream like a tiny, detached iceberg. Elizabeth imagined if her feet were in the icy water.

Her father saw her shiver and put his arm round her. 'What are you thinking?'

She smiled. For as long as she could remember, he had asked the same question. 'How unbearably cold it must be in the water,' she replied.

He told her that waterbirds have colder blood in their feet than in the rest of their bodies, so it wouldn't bother them. She wasn't so sure. She imagined the shock of being submerged in the river, and pressed against him. He laughed and put her over his shoulder in a fireman's lift.

'Put me down!' she cried, pounding his back with her fists and laughing as the snow jumped off his wax jacket.

After they returned inside, the snow started to fall again, and before long the garden was pristine, like the surface of a swimming pool at night.

When Elizabeth came down for breakfast the next morning, her parents were looking out onto the garden. They stopped talking when they saw her.

'What's the matter?'

Mary smiled and asked what she wanted to eat.

'Dad? What is it?'

Tom looked at Mary, who shook her head. He sighed. 'Just someone with a poor sense of humour,' he said.

Elizabeth walked over and stood with them at the window. The snow had continued to fall heavily overnight and the shrubs in the garden stooped under the weight. The lawn was submerged in an immaculate white duvet, inches thick, that was as smooth as fresh plaster. And then she saw it, written in the snow: 'WE ARE WAITING FOR YOU'.

They considered calling the police. After rehearsing what they would say, they decided it sounded ridiculous. No crime had been committed and the police would no doubt suggest it was just a joke. But there was still something about it that bothered Mary and she couldn't get it out of her head. When Tom asked what it was, she could only say that it didn't 'feel right'. And the more she thought about it, the more elusive the answer became.

Mary went to the front of the house and looked onto the street and the cars that had become shapeless with snow. She watched two strangers walk past with a dog. They left different-shaped footprints on the path. 'Tom, I've got it!' She ran back into the kitchen. When she saw Elizabeth, she thought better of it and half-heartedly suggested that they all build a snowman.

Tom laughed and played along. 'Maybe later. It's too cold out there now,' he said.

Elizabeth laughed too and gave her mother a hug before going over to the fridge.

Mary took her husband's arm and pulled him over to the window, out of earshot. 'The message in the snow, Tom. I know what was so strange about it.'

He glanced at Elizabeth to make sure she wasn't listening. 'Tell me.'

'There are no footprints.'

Father David Montague was walking the short distance from his home to the church. It had been over twenty years since he'd witnessed the car accident that had led to him joining the ministry. He had left his notebook in the vestry and needed to look through it before tomorrow. He entered the church porch and felt around with the long iron key until it caught in the lock.

'Father, I need your help.'

A figure sat on one of the stone benches in the porch. The man's head was bowed and his face was shrouded by a hood. The priest's pulse quickened. He always worried about thieves breaking into the church.

'It's very late; perhaps we could talk in the morning?' He was puzzled as to why he hadn't seen the man sooner.

'I wasn't aware the ministry had opening hours,' the stranger replied.

Thinking that he could ring the bells to attract attention if he was attacked, Father Montague suggested they go inside and talk.

'I can't go in, Father,' the man said. 'We can talk here.'

'What is it you want from me?'

'I am looking for someone.'

'And who is that?'

'A child in grave danger. I thought you might know her.' The man's eyes searched Montague's for clues. 'I don't know her name. She has golden hair and lives nearby.'

The priest's throat was dry and he swallowed before taking a deep breath. 'Right, that's it. I'm calling the police. They can sort this out,' he blustered. He marched to the gate between the cemetery and vicarage before glancing over his shoulder. He jumped when a voice called out in front of him.

'It is your duty to help me, Father.' The man was standing on the other side of the gate, cutting off his escape route.

Montague turned again and ran back to the church, catching the heel of his shoe in the hem of his cassock and losing his footing on the icy path. He fell head first, grazing his hands and striking his head on the edge of a paving stone. Blood ran into his eyes, and he blinked to try and clear them. He knew he would have only moments before his pursuer was upon him. He cried out and pushed himself up to reach the final few yards to the church door. Making it inside, he drew the bolt and rested his back against the timbers to catch his breath. Then he realised he wasn't alone. Slow, deliberate footsteps made their way down the steps by the pulpit. 'Thank the Lord,' he gasped.

'Father Montague, I wanted to rehearse before tomorrow. I wasn't expecting to see you. Whatever has happened to your head?' the church organist asked, shocked to see that he was hurt.

'I fear we may have an intruder, Mrs Gapper, and I don't have time to explain. I need your help to raise the alarm.'

She told him she didn't have a mobile phone, so they

headed for the bell tower. Montague gave a silent prayer, hoping someone would wonder why the bells were ringing in the middle of the day.

That afternoon, Mary persuaded Elizabeth to accompany her to the shops. Once Tom heard them shut the front gate, he walked into town himself, careful to take a different route. His appointment was at 4pm. He went through the front door of the police station exactly on the hour.

The duty officer didn't appear concerned when he heard what had happened. He escorted Tom into a private room and introduced him to Detective Constable Amanda Roberts. As Tom answered her questions, it occurred to him that he had no proof that Elizabeth had met anyone those two times she'd left the house at night. He may consider it out of character, but a sense of adventure and a vivid imagination are a potent cocktail, the policewoman pointed out.

When he left the station half an hour later, he felt foolish for having wasted their time. Needing to clear his head, he walked out of town to the lock. The fresh air and exercise helped ease his embarrassment and gave him time to think. Of course, he had no evidence that Elizabeth was slipping out to meet anyone. He did know his daughter, though, and he was certain that something traumatic had happened to her and someone else was involved. He watched a barge grumbling against the current, the smoke from its stove clinging to the underside of the bridge, before he carried on across the river and set off along the footpath on the other side.

He thought about who else could help him get to the bottom of it. Simon Pankhurst would be a good start, so he decided to work from home on Monday and take Elizabeth to school. He would then try and pull her teacher to one side. The days were short now and he could pick out cyclists along the towpath by their lights. Before he went home, he had someone else to visit. He sent Mary a message, letting her know. Among his duties as parish priest, Father Montague was also the chaplain at Elizabeth's school and Tom thought he might know of someone called Tobias. If the priest wasn't at the church, he was likely to be at the vicarage next door.

Tom heard the bells as he was walking alongside a high red-brick wall that led to the church. That was a good sign that Montague was there, so he was surprised to find the entrance to the church locked. The bells were still ringing, so he walked around the building, trying to find another way in. The rear door was also locked. He peered in one of the windows. Whoever was inside must be in the bell tower, which was hidden from view. He returned to the front of the church and pounded the door with his fist. The bells were too loud, so he tried again with his foot and called out for Father Montague. There was a pause in the ringing, so he kicked the door harder and shouted. The bells stayed silent and he heard footsteps.

'Father? It's Tom Fairchild.'

'Are you alone?' the voice replied from behind the door.

'Of course I'm alone,' Tom snapped. 'Open the bloody door.'

There was a soft thud and it opened.

'What's going on? Has someone attacked you, Father?'

The priest motioned for him to come in and locked the door again. Tom saw the church organist peer round the side of the curtain dividing the nave from the bell tower.

'Mrs Gapper?'

'She helped me ring the bells, Tom. We have an emergency.' Montague told him about the stranger and how, fearing for his safety, he had retreated to the sanctuary of the church to raise the alarm. He had then fallen and hit his head. 'Thankfully, you came quickly.'

'Why on earth didn't you call the police?'

'I don't carry a phone and Mrs Gapper left hers in the car.'

Tom shook his head, then told them he hadn't seen anyone outside. He also hadn't noticed anyone as he'd walked over. He then explained that he hadn't actually come because the bells were ringing. Rather, he wanted to talk to Montague about Elizabeth.

'Then perhaps you were heaven sent after all,' Father Montague said, before explaining what the stranger had said to him.

'And you think he was looking for Elizabeth?'

'She was the first person I thought of, Tom.'

'That's ridiculous! There must be loads of fair-haired children living round here.'

'Well, he said a girl, for a start,' the priest said. 'And given what you just told me about her disappearance the other night, it does seem a rather worrying coincidence.'

'What else did he say?'

'That she was in grave danger.'

'From him, by the sound of it,' Tom sneered.

'I don't know. There was certainly something disturbing about him. And yet, if he means her harm, it would seem a little odd to come to the church for help finding her.'

Tom started to pace while he thought and then shook his head.

'There is something else. Walk with me, back to the house. I have something to show you.'

They escorted the organist to her car, then headed for the vicarage. As they walked, Tom could see that Father Montague was still shaken and repeatedly looked over his shoulder. When they were inside the house, the priest made sure the ground-floor doors and windows were secured. It had started to rain, and the water was already filling the gutters and running down the drainpipes before pooling on the ground. He drew the curtains and put the kettle on. His wife joined them in the kitchen.

'Catherine, you know Tom, don't you?'

'Yes, of course. Tom, how are you?'

Tom nodded. 'I'm OK, but I can't say the same for your husband.'

She looked at Montague and gasped. 'What have you done, David?'

'It's nothing, just a bit of blood. I tripped outside the church.'

'Let me clean it up for you,' she said, putting a paper kitchen towel under the tap. She told him to hold still as she wiped dried blood from the wound. 'It's just a scratch,' she said, kissing him on the cheek. 'Now, who wants a cup of tea?' The kettle had boiled and she lined up three mugs.

'Actually, I might need something stronger,' Montague said, trying to laugh.

Catherine stopped and looked at them. 'All right, you two. Who's going to tell me what's going on?'

'Something strange just happened, Catherine. There was a man I didn't know waiting outside the church. He said he needed my help finding someone.'

'Is he there now?' she asked, looking towards the window.

'No, I think he's gone. But he said he was looking for a girl who's in danger.'

'What sort of danger?'

'I don't know. I didn't give him chance to explain.' Montague looked at the floor. 'He said he didn't know who she was other than that she lived nearby and had golden hair.'

Tom saw Catherine glance his way, before asking her husband if he had really fallen over.

Montague laughed more easily this time. 'Yes, I really did. I wasn't attacked. I have to confess I was trying to get away from him at the time.'

'I think you should call the police.'

'Hold on a minute,' Tom said. 'I really don't see what the police are expected to do about this. He fell and hurt himself. It wasn't this man's fault. He hasn't actually done anything other than creep you out,' he added, looking at Montague. Tom then told them how the police had made him feel foolish earlier that afternoon after he had gone to the station.

Montague closed his eyes and pinched the top of his nose with his fingers, then sat down at the kitchen table. 'Perhaps I will have that tea, Catherine,' he said.

'You said you had something to show me,' Tom reminded him.

For a moment, Montague looked confused. 'Oh yes, I'm sorry,' he said, before getting up again and walking through to the sitting room.

When he was gone, Tom turned to Catherine. 'And I don't see why you think Elizabeth is the only girl around here with golden hair.'

'I didn't say that…'

Father Montague came back into the room and put a box file on the table. 'This has sat on our bookcase since we moved in,' he said, leaning over to blow dust off the cover. 'It was such a shock at the time that my predecessor kept it in plain view so he would never forget. I've maintained the tradition.' He pressed the clasp to unfasten it and lifted the cover, handing Tom a faded cutting from the local newspaper. 'When I came to the parish twenty-five years ago, the old vicar left behind this scrapbook of newspaper cuttings and church notices. When you were telling me about Elizabeth, I had a strange sense of déjà vu.'

Tom ignored him and read the newspaper headline: 'Local girl still missing – police search riverbank'. He looked at the date. 'This was fifty years ago! What's it got to do with Elizabeth?' He dropped the newspaper cutting onto the table.

Montague produced a second article from the box file.

Tom read as far as the opening paragraph before this time bringing his fist down on the table, spilling their cups of tea. 'Are you telling me we have a predator out there targeting local girls with blonde hair?' he shouted. He re-read the opening paragraph again.

Police have scaled down their search for missing schoolgirl Cassandra Porter after failing to find a body or make any arrests. The teenager went missing six weeks ago on the night of 13th April after failing to return home from school. Anyone with any information as to her whereabouts should contact Detective Inspector Barry Simmonds of the Metropolitan Police. She was last seen wearing her school clothes and has distinctive shoulder-length blonde hair.

'What in God's name is going on?'

'I'm sure it's just a coincidence,' Montague replied, wiping up the spilled tea. 'And it was a long time ago. Whoever took Cassandra Porter, assuming she was abducted and didn't just run away or fall in the river, would be an old man now.' He paused. 'For some reason it occurred to me after what you told me. And my visitor's preoccupation with the girl's hair colour today was particularly odd when you think about it.'

Tom shook his head. 'Well, I'm not thinking about it any more.' He got up and nodded goodbye to Catherine before telling them he was going for a drink.

'Didn't you say in the church that you had something to ask me, Tom?' Montague called after him.

Tom was at the door when he turned to answer. 'Do you know a boy called Tobias?'

Montague thought for a moment. 'I actually don't, Tom, no. Why?'

'It doesn't matter,' Tom said, wishing them both a good night.

After he had gone, Father Montague told Catherine again, in detail, what had happened at the church, then opened the kitchen drawer and took out a large, heavy-duty torch and checked the battery. He then went into the porch and lifted his coat off the hook.

'Where are you going?'

'If Tom won't listen, then perhaps Mary will.'

'I do think you should just call the police.'

'And tell them what? Tom's right. A man came to the church looking for someone. That's all. We don't have his name and we can't be sure who he was looking for. And, of course, then I got scared, ran away and fell over.'

'When you put it like that…' Catherine smiled. 'But you could at least suggest that Tom mentions it to the police officer he spoke to earlier.'

'I'll do that,' Montague said. 'But I'll work on Mary first while he is at the pub.' He kissed Catherine on the cheek. 'Lock the door when I've gone.' He wiped condensation off one of the small panes of glass in the back door and looked to make sure the coast was clear. All he could see in the gloom were the trees that overhung misshapen, decaying gravestones. He turned the key in the lock and stepped out into the rain.

ELEVEN

Tobias Mallory

After leaving the vicarage, Tom changed his mind about going for a drink. Even though he was irritated that Montague and his wife assumed that the stranger was looking for Elizabeth, part of him worried that they could be right, so he was uncomfortable staying out any longer. When he drew level with the pub, the rain was heavier, so he broke into a jog. When he got home, he took off his coat and boots in the porch, then went to look for a bottle of wine. Mary asked why he had been so long and he said he would explain once he'd got them both a drink.

'There's been a bit of drama up at the church I'll tell you about.'

The moment the cork popped free of the bottle, there was a knock at the door. Tom rarely saw benefit in answering the front door in the early evening, unless he was expecting someone. Tonight, he wanted to know who was out there. What he didn't expect to find was a Benedictine monk. The man's face was cast in shadow from his hood and he held his hands in front of him in prayer. When he didn't speak immediately, Tom asked what he wanted.

'I've come for your daughter.'

'I'm sorry?' Tom spluttered.

'She is in danger. If you don't let me protect her, you will lose her.'

'What are you talking about? Who are you?'

'I'm sorry, Tom. He must have waited at the church.' Father Montague approached the house.

The monk's gaze never left Tom.

'What the hell is going on here?' Tom demanded.

Mary now stood alongside him, holding his arm. 'What is it, Tom? What's the matter?'

'That's what I'm trying to find out. Father Montague appears to have brought this man to our door who says Elizabeth is in some sort of danger.'

'He must have followed you, Tom,' Montague explained. 'I was coming over to see if Mary could persuade you to speak to the police again.'

'I don't understand,' Mary said. 'You've already been to see the police today, haven't you, Tom?'

Ignoring her, Tom stepped towards the monk. 'What do you mean, our daughter's in danger?' he demanded, his voice breaking.

'Is she here now?' the monk asked.

'Mary, call the police. I'll watch him,' Tom said, ushering her back into the house.

'No one else can help you,' the monk replied. 'Perhaps, before doing anything, you might check she is safe.'

Tom looked back at Mary, who turned for the stairs, calling Elizabeth's name. The house fell silent.

'Mary? Have you got her?' Tom's voice rose in pitch.

'She's not here!' his wife yelled.

'Tell me where my daughter is or I'll break every bone in your body,' Tom growled.

The monk tilted his head to one side. 'The house in the woods,' he said. 'They'll take her there. If we're lucky, she isn't there yet.' He looked up and, through a break in the clouds, there appeared a pristine full moon. 'We must hurry. There isn't much time.'

'Wait a minute; get back here,' Tom demanded. He looked at Montague in desperation and then grabbed his coat from the hook.

The monk had turned the corner in the road towards the river and was now out of sight. They ran after him.

'Where did he go? He could only have been twenty yards in front of us and now he's disappeared!'

'Could he be on a boat?' Montague asked, looking out over the water.

'Yes – over there!' Tom shouted, pointing in the direction of a clearing on the far bank.

They saw the shape of a man in a cloak preparing to land.

'Come on – my outboard is over there.' Tom untied the boat from its mooring and gunned the motor into life, taking less than a minute to cross the river. After fastening it next to the other boat, they looked in each direction along the towpath, then headed after the monk into Nightshade Wood.

'The path continues past that tree,' Montague said, pointing. 'He must have gone up there.'

It had stopped raining and the ground was slippery. They had to be careful not to lose their footing. Before long, they reached a fork in the path.

'Now what?' Tom asked.

They stopped to listen for any movement.

'Tom, I wonder if—'

'Shh – what was that?' Tom asked, turning his head to where the sound had come from. 'I thought I heard something.'

They remained still and listened. There was a tremendous crash from two branches coming together that echoed through the woods.

'This way,' Tom said, taking the right-hand fork in the path.

As they ran, undergrowth tugged at their feet and shins, slowing them down. Small branches caught and tore at their hands and faces and snagged their clothing.

'There he is!' shouted Tom.

The priest caught up with him, then they both stopped. The monk had his back to them and raised his arm as if gesturing to someone. He was half the length of a football pitch away. If they ran hard, they could be with him in moments. Before they could move, he disappeared behind a yew tree that glistened with cobwebs on the tips of its dark-green needles.

'Hey, you – get back here!' shouted Tom, breaking into a sprint.

When they reached the tree, there was a muffled thump, and a clump of mud flew into the air as Tom kicked the ground in frustration.

'This is a nightmare; I can't believe it's happening,' he howled.

Montague bent down and put his hands on his knees to catch his breath. Sweat dripped off the tip of his chin as he tried to make sense of what was going on.

Mary saw the flashing blue light reflected in the window of the house over the road and opened her front door. A breeze blew her thick dark hair across her face, forcing her to pull the loose strands behind her ears. Two plain clothes police officers got out of the car and slammed the doors. The first to the doorstep had long brown hair tied in a ponytail.

'Mrs Fairchild? I'm DC Roberts. Can we come in?'

Mary showed them through to the living room. 'Thank you for coming so quickly. It's our daughter, Elizabeth. She's missing.'

'When did you last see her?'

'We got back from town together at around 5pm. Although it's half-term, she had homework to do, so she went up to her room. Now she's nowhere in the house.'

'So she's been missing for about an hour?'

Mary nodded.

'You mentioned you had a visitor tonight.'

'Yes, it was really strange. He was dressed like a monk and he came to the door just before Father Montague and told my husband, Tom, that Elizabeth was in danger. He said to go and check on her. When I did, she wasn't there.'

'Then what happened?'

Mary explained the sequence of events and how her husband and the priest had left with the visitor.

'Which woods are we talking about?'

'I've no idea. All the monk said was "the white house in the woods". They set off on foot, so I can only imagine it's Nightshade, which is the closest wood to us on the other side of the river.'

'I'm not aware of any monasteries around here. Can you describe him?'

'Not really, apart from the habit he was wearing. It was black and looked very basic, like it was made from hessian, and tied with rope around the waist,' Mary said. 'His face was in shadow.'

'So what's Father Montague got to do with all of this?' asked DC Roberts.

'He told us he had encountered the man this afternoon outside the church,' Mary replied. 'The monk asked him if he knew of a local girl with golden hair.'

'And you think he had already identified Elizabeth and was looking for her?' asked the other officer.

'Well, I don't know. What do you think?'

Roberts put her hand on Mary's arm reassuringly and said they would do all they could to find Elizabeth. 'Is it possible she went out with friends and didn't tell you?' she asked.

'She would never do that. We're always reminding her of the importance of letting us know where she is. And besides, she's too young to go out and play at this time of year.'

'But she has done this before, hasn't she?'

'Well, not really,' Mary protested. 'She's wandered down to the river a couple of times. Nothing like this.'

As the questions continued, Mary looked past the police officers and out the window at the orange street light and wondered where her husband was with Father Montague.

'We've lost them, but there is someone who can help.'

Tom and Montague saw the monk.

'Find Cornelius Draper. He is in the street to the north of here. There is a grotesque above his door.' The monk then backed away and disappeared through a tangle of bushes.

135

'What?!' Tom shouted after him, before turning to Montague. 'Have you any idea what the hell he's talking about?'

'I think I might, actually,' Montague replied. 'There's a row of Georgian houses on the other side of these woods. It's not far; we can be there in fifteen minutes if we hurry. And when he says a grotesque, I think he means a gargoyle. So we should be able to find it.'

After leaving the woods, they hurried down the road before taking a narrow cut-through to the street of Georgian houses. They checked the front door of each house.

'I know! I think it's down here on the right,' Montague said.

'I thought you said you didn't know this Draper?' Tom asked.

'I don't. However, I do remember seeing a grotesque iron knocker on the door of one of these houses just a little further up. The only thing…' Montague paused.

'What?' asked Tom.

'Well,' Montague continued, 'I thought the house was empty. I always assumed nobody lived there.'

'We'll soon find out,' Tom replied, marching past him and the line of evergreen shrubs at the front of the houses.

'This is the one,' Montague called out, pointing to a five-storey terraced house towards the far end of the row.

As the men approached, they saw a front garden overgrown with weeds and climbers, and the windows had a dull pallor that contrasted with the crisp glint from the other houses.

'It's as I remembered. It doesn't look like anyone's home. If you look, there is a gargoyle on the front door,' Montague said.

Tom flinched when something touched his leg, then put his hand to his pocket when he realised that the vibration was his phone. It was Mary.

'She's home, Tom.'

When Elizabeth came downstairs the next morning, the kitchen was silent. Tom sat at the table eating a piece of toast, while Mary stood with her back to the room, looking out into the garden.

'Good morning,' Elizabeth said meekly.

'How are you feeling?' Tom asked, his voice flat.

'Fine, thanks. Just a little tired.' She looked over at Mary. 'Mum?'

Mary's shoulders moved but she didn't reply. Elizabeth walked over and touched her on the arm, and saw that she was crying.

'Mummy, what is it?'

Mary turned to face her, the tears now rolling down her face. 'Elizabeth, from the day you were born, your father and I have done everything we could to keep you safe. Your well-being is all that matters to us, and if anything happened to you, our lives would be over.' Saying the words proved too much and she began weeping uncontrollably.

'Look, Mum—'

'No, you listen to your mother!' Tom shouted.

Mary continued. 'The last week has been the worst of our lives,' she said between sobs. 'And what has made it worse is that you care so little about us that you won't say what you were doing.'

Elizabeth mumbled at the floor.

'What was that?' Tom asked.

'I can't,' she replied, a little louder.

'You can't?!' he thundered.

'I made a promise not to tell anyone.'

He slammed both fists into the kitchen table and stood up. Next to his plate, a jar of marmalade tipped onto its side and rolled in a slow-motion arc before smashing on the floor.

'Tom, no,' Mary implored.

He glared at Elizabeth, then looked down at the mess on the floor and swore.

Mary took the opportunity to take over. 'Darling, if someone has told you not to tell us what happened, then you need to think why they would do that and what they have to hide.'

Before Elizabeth could answer, there was a knock at the door. Tom pushed his chair back across the floor and strode past her into the hall. She and Mary heard talking but couldn't hear who was there.

'Come in, Mr Pankhurst; perhaps you can make her see some sense.' Tom came back into the kitchen, followed by Elizabeth's teacher.

'Hello, Mrs Fairchild, Elizabeth.' Simon Pankhurst smiled, nodding to each.

Elizabeth blushed.

'Your parents told me there was a bit of excitement last night so I thought I should come and see how you are.'

Mary asked if he wanted a cup of tea and put the kettle on.

Tom pulled out a chair for him and told Elizabeth to join them at the table. 'Thank you for coming over,' he said to the teacher. 'The last week has been unsettling for all of us, so we appreciate your support.'

Pankhurst smiled again and looked at Elizabeth. 'How are you?' he asked.

'I'm absolutely fine!' she replied, shaking her head. 'I don't see why everyone's so stressed out over this. I just went out for a few hours and lost track of the time.'

Mary looked at Tom, urging him not to say anything. Pankhurst changed tack and asked Elizabeth how she was finding school. He asked if she was having any problems with the other children. When she was reluctant to answer, he looked over to her parents, who took the hint and left the room.

After they had gone, he tried again. 'You and I have a good relationship at school, Elizabeth, and you know you can trust me, don't you?'

When she didn't reply, he repeated the question.

'Yes.'

'Yes, what?'

'Yes, Mr Pankhurst.'

He laughed and she looked up.

'That wasn't what I meant,' he said, still smiling. 'I would like you to convince me that you do in fact trust me.'

She nodded, then said quietly, 'I do trust you.'

'Good. Then you know I wouldn't betray your confidence. So tell me: who is upsetting you at school?'

She looked down and shook her head.

'Elizabeth, please.'

'It's no one at school.' She looked up at him. 'Really, it's not. Some of them are a bit weird but they've nothing to do with this.'

'I can't argue with that,' Pankhurst said. 'Just don't tell anyone I said that. And thank you for confiding in me. I'm relieved no one else at school is involved. Now, you know what my next question is.'

She looked at him and nodded. 'Mr Pankhurst, you know how you wouldn't...' she paused, remembering his words, 'betray my confidence?'

'Absolutely.'

'Well, I too have been asked to keep a secret, which means I can't tell you.'

He rolled his eyes and sighed. 'Elizabeth, this is different. At school, I am your guardian, and you trust me to keep you safe and have your best interests at heart. Anybody who takes you away from your home and those who love you, and encourages you to lie about it, is unworthy of your trust.'

'He hasn't encouraged me to lie.'

'Who hasn't?'

'The person you're talking about,' she replied. 'He hasn't asked me to lie to anyone.'

'What has he asked you to do, then?'

'He doesn't want anyone to know where we go or what happens there.'

'Would you at least tell me his name?' Pankhurst asked, not expecting an answer.

'Tobias Mallory.'

On the other side of the door, Tom looked at his wife. 'I don't believe it!' he hissed, shaking his head.

'In her dream, she was calling out for someone and I thought she said, "Tobias". But when I mentioned it, she said she didn't know anyone by that name,' Mary said.

She squeezed his hand and whispered that it was a good sign because it meant that Elizabeth's teacher was getting to the truth. He nodded and they continued listening.

'Tobias Mallory? That's quite an unusual name. Definitely not a boy at the school. How old is he?'

Elizabeth shrugged. 'I actually haven't asked him. He looks around my age: eleven.'

'And what does he look like?'

'Why do you want to know?'

'In case I have seen him myself.'

Elizabeth shook her head. 'I don't want to talk about him any more.'

After a pause, her parents came back into the room and exchanged nods with Pankhurst. He stayed long enough to tell Elizabeth that he was available whenever she was ready to speak again and wished them all a good day. Elizabeth used his departure to leave the kitchen herself and headed upstairs to her bedroom. Mary and Tom decided to give her some space and let her go. They were relieved at last to have something to go on and a name they could share with the police. Tom sat at the bottom of the stairs to think. Tobias Mallory. Could it be a pseudonym? Was Elizabeth really telling the truth? He didn't know any Mallorys. He left a message for the detective and then called Father Montague.

'Do you know the name Mallory?'

'Mallory…' Montague repeated and looked at his wife. She shook her head, but he said it was familiar.

'Specifically, a boy named Tobias Mallory.'

'Oh, *that* Tobias.'

'So you do know him?'

'No, sorry, Tom. I meant, I see what you're talking about. You asked me last night if I knew a Tobias and now you have a surname.'

'That's right. And you thought you knew the name?'

'The name Mallory, yes; not Tobias.'

'Then what is familiar about it?'

Father Montague thought for a moment. 'Can you come over?'

When Tom arrived at the vicarage, Montague was waiting outside.

'Sorry to drag you over here, Tom. I have something else to show you again.' As they walked through the churchyard, he apologised in case it wasn't much help. 'There,' he said, pointing at a large family gravestone. It was green with age and leaning at an angle. 'I don't know anyone else by that name.'

Tom lifted his hand to keep the rain out of his eyes and tried to make out the faded inscription. 'I can't read it. I see the name Mallory but nothing else. Perhaps a date: 17 or 1886; I'm not sure.'

'Me neither,' replied Montague. 'However, it shows that there was a family of that name living around here at one time.'

'But not any more?'

'Tom, I don't know. I don't recognise the name from our congregation or from the school. What did Elizabeth tell you?'

Tom told him what had happened and that he had just left a message for the detective.

'Well, if anyone can trace the family, the police should be able to,' Montague said.

Tom nodded and told him that he would call with news, and thanked him for his help looking for Elizabeth last night. 'And if that weirdo turns up here again, make sure you've got a mobile with you this time and call the police, then me,' Tom added.

When Montague got home, Catherine asked what had happened. He told her about the gravestone, then sat down and took out the newspaper cutting about the missing girl from nearly fifty years ago.

'Do you really think these events are related?'

'I really don't know, Catherine. I do have a horrible feeling about it all. I can only pray I'm wrong.'

With half-term over, Elizabeth decided to drop by Maurice Truman's room on her way to assembly. She had been pleased to see him at the river and was happy to have someone with whom to share her secret adventures. When she got there, his door was closed. She knocked, then tried calling his name. When there was still no reply, she raised her fist to try for a third time. Then Simon Pankhurst appeared beside her.

'Elizabeth, we need to go upstairs. It's important no-one's late this morning.'

She did as she was told and followed him up the winding stone steps to the school hall. Once inside, a murmur went up and she was surprised to see the head teacher walk in, which was unusual for a midweek assembly. She told them all to sit down, as she had some sad news to share.

When she heard that Maurice was dead, Elizabeth found it hard to breathe. Her head felt light and she was having difficulty concentrating on what Mrs Cuthbertson was saying. She did hear that Maurice had passed away yesterday, unexpectedly, and the school would provide counselling for those who needed it. She couldn't remember anything else apart from a mention of a police investigation, which the head teacher said was normal in such circumstances. Elizabeth tried to let the words sink in. A police investigation. Could that mean it wasn't natural causes? Mrs Cuthbertson told them that she expected to have funeral details next week and hoped everyone would make an effort to attend. Elizabeth felt numb, and wanted to get up and run. How long after she saw him last night did Maurice die? Was it at home or on the river? Was it an accident or did someone attack him? She thought of the ferryman and his horrible face. Poor Maurice. Then she began to cry and the tears filled her eyes and hung on her lashes, before rolling down her cheeks. It was contagious and the assembly was soon filled with the sound of crying.

The teachers decided that the best thing to do was to get the pupils some fresh air and ushered them towards the door. Pankhurst went over to comfort Elizabeth. He was surprised by her reaction as she rarely showed emotion. Then he remembered that she had tried to visit the caretaker before assembly. When she saw him, she gave in completely and he watched her shoulders rise and fall in time with great racking sobs. He bent down and put an arm around her, lifting her out of her seat and walking her to the end of the aisle and then the door. When they were downstairs, he escorted her towards a walnut tree that stood watch outside the church. They sat at its foot, resting their backs against its smooth bark.

'Are you OK?' He had drawn one knee up to his chest and stretched out his other leg, letting the outer edge of a scruffy black lace-up rest against the gravel. 'You know, Elizabeth, it is shocking and sad what's happened to Maurice, but he hadn't been in very good health and these things can happen when people get older.'

As soon as the words had left his mouth, he knew his attempt at comforting her was clumsy. Her face remained pressed into shaking forearms that pulled her knees up tight to her chest.

He tried again. 'I didn't realise you were close to him.'

This time, he got a response. 'I wasn't,' she replied.

'Well, it's unusual for pupils to visit the caretaker. Remember I spoke to you before assembly, outside his room?'

She nodded, not looking up. He allowed silence to apply its own pressure.

'I just wanted to say hello,' she offered. 'I wanted to talk to him…' She let the words tail off.

'Elizabeth, I know I'm your teacher; however, I hope one day you can see me as a friend. Until that time, as I said to you before, I would be grateful if you would at least trust that I am on your side and want to help.'

She took a deep breath and said, 'I bumped into Mo one night last week on the river and wanted to talk to him about it today, that's all.'

Pankhurst was shocked to hear that the caretaker's death had coincided with Elizabeth's disappearance. 'Do you mean *on* the river or *by* it?' he asked.

She thought he was correcting her grammar and was annoyed. 'If you were in a boat, Mr Pankhurst, would it be fair to say you were also *on* the river, or would you be *by* it?' The moment she answered, she realised her mistake.

'What were you doing on the river at night?! And when exactly did you see Mr Truman? Elizabeth, we need to tell the police about this.'

She thought quickly for a way out. Telling her parents would be disastrous and talking to the police even worse.

They were trained in getting to the truth and would then tell her parents. There was only one thing for it. She lifted her head to look at her teacher. 'Oh, Mr Pankhurst, I'm so sorry,' she gushed and threw her arms around his neck.

He put his arms out behind him on the ground for support to prevent falling backwards. After regaining his balance, he patted her on the back to break the embrace. 'It's OK,' he said, 'just tell me what happened.'

'You're quite right, of course,' she began. 'I was by the river when I saw Mr Truman. It was the evening I was coming back from Freddie's house.'

'You were at Freddie's house?'

'Briefly, yes,' she lied. 'I called to borrow a book he had mentioned.'

'Oh really, which one?'

She was pleased with herself for introducing an element of truth to her story, as Freddie had indeed lent her a book over half-term. What was not true was her seeing Maurice Truman the same evening. She told the teacher about the book and mentioned a particular episode that she had enjoyed, and that seemed to convince him.

They parted, with him offering to give her a private lesson next week to discuss the book, while telling her that she could call him any time to talk about Maurice. She thanked him and left the churchyard, relieved but still devastated at the news. She now needed to talk to someone she could trust and, given the circumstances, it would have to be Tobias.

TWELVE

Digging for Clues

Barry Simmonds had joined the Metropolitan Police force as the 1950s ended. He'd made detective two years later, and six years after that was the officer in charge of the Cassandra Porter case. After taking early retirement in 1990, he'd sold his home and moved to a small bungalow close to the coast, from where it was a short walk to the allotments on the outskirts of the town. It was there, among the rows of vegetables and makeshift scarecrows and empty strings of tin cans, that Simmonds had agreed to meet Tom and Father Montague. The priest had offered to try and set up a meeting with the retired detective after Tom had become frustrated at the lack of interest from the local force.

The drive from London took two hours and they were relieved to pass the sign for the 'historic market town' of Lewes, twinned with places they hadn't heard of in France and Germany. Tom was grateful that Simmonds had agreed to see them. He was also relieved that the old man was still alive.

'I suppose he had left the force when you came to the parish?' Tom asked.

'Yes, he was well before my time,' explained Montague. 'A man called Turner was in charge of the boys in blue when I moved here. He's retired too now, of course, but he remained in the area. Simmonds was his first DI and they still exchange Christmas cards, which is how I got his telephone number.'

Tom turned off the main road and parked alongside a chestnut-pale perimeter fence. 'Odd place to meet,' he muttered.

Montague smiled as they opened the car doors and looked for the entrance to the allotment. A couple with a small dog emerged from the field up the track, so the men headed in that direction. They entered the code they had been given for the gate and proceeded up the path, looking for a shed off to the right with a cockerel weathervane on the roof. They heard it creaking before they saw it.

'There it is, Tom.'

They moved off the main path, past a row of cabbages, and saw the retired policeman in a low canvas chair, his eyes closed and his face raised to enjoy the last of the winter sun.

'Detective Inspector Simmonds?'

Simmonds wore a thick miner's coat and dirt-flecked cords, and didn't respond.

'Excuse me?' Montague tried again, a little louder.

There was a snort and Simmonds opened one eye. He pushed himself up using his elbows and cleared his throat. 'I'm sorry, I must've nodded off. Father Montague and Tom Fairchild, I presume?'

'You have a good memory for names,' Tom remarked.

Simmonds smiled and motioned for them to sit. 'So you want to know about Cassandra Porter?'

'That's right, Mr Simmonds. I was telling Tom how I inherited a box of cuttings from my predecessor at St Anne's that included some newspaper reports about the missing girl.'

'May I ask why the interest?' Simmonds said to Tom. He had not been a policeman for many years and his face was weathered from spending time outside. Grey wisps of hair poked out from under a tweed cap and his gaze made Tom feel uncomfortable.

'It's about Tom's daughter—' Montague said.

'No, Father, let me explain,' Tom interrupted. 'My daughter, Elizabeth, went missing last Thursday night. We found her in the early hours by the river. She claims not to remember anything that happened to her. The reason we've come to see you is: my wife and I had a visitor the evening Elizabeth disappeared who warned us she was in danger. And it wasn't until he came to the house that we realised Elizabeth was missing.'

'I see. And you think there's a connection with what happened to Cassandra?'

'I wanted your opinion on that, actually,' Tom admitted. 'There are similarities. Let me show you a photograph of Elizabeth.' He took out his phone.

'There's certainly a resemblance,' Simmonds said, looking all of his eighty-plus years. 'Cassie had the most stunning long flaxen hair. But there are so many missing persons reports each year, and some of those are girls and some have blonde hair. What makes you think these two incidents are related?'

Montague stepped forward. 'Mr Simmonds, there's more you need to know. The man who warned us that

Elizabeth was in danger wanted to find her himself. He first visited me at the church earlier that afternoon with a description of a girl he was looking for and he was very specific about the colour of her hair. At that stage, he didn't know Elizabeth's name or where she lived. I'm telling you this in case there are similarities with Cassandra's disappearance.'

'I take it you don't have his name?'

They shook their heads.

'So what did he look like?'

'I know it sounds ridiculous. He appeared to be a monk,' Montague said. 'He was certainly dressed like one.'

The old man went to speak, but no words came out. He brought a handkerchief to his mouth and his chest rose as he breathed more heavily.

'Are you all right?' Tom asked.

Simmonds nodded and took his hand from his face. 'When Cassandra Porter went missing, we must've taken witness statements from damn near everyone in the town. One that always stuck with me was the lady who used to have the bakers next to the old post office. She told us that someone had been in, asking about a girl who matched the description of Cassie.'

Tom looked at Father Montague.

'Go on, Barry,' the priest said.

'We did look into what she had told us. It led to a dead end too,' Simmonds explained, before pausing. 'Except the man she said came into her shop that day was a monk.'

Tom felt the hairs rise on the back of his neck. 'That doesn't make any sense, though, does it?' he asked. 'How old was the man she saw?'

'He was young. She thought he looked in his late twenties,' Simmonds remembered.

'Well, then, it can't be the same man,' said Father Montague, 'as that would put him in his sixties now. And the man we saw could have been no more than thirty himself.'

They fell silent and listened to a wood pigeon on the far side of the allotment call for its partner. There was a flutter of wings and a robin landed on the gutter of the shed.

'Bit of a coincidence, though, isn't it?' Tom said. 'And why didn't the woman's statement lead anywhere?'

'We had no other reports of a man matching his description and there hasn't been a religious order in the area for hundreds of years. So if he really was a monk, then he wasn't local, which means he could've come from anywhere.'

Montague cleared his throat. 'Well, you do have another report of a man matching his description now, don't you, Mr Simmonds?'

The retired detective pushed down on the armrests of his chair and stood up. His face was flushed. 'Well, I have a question for the both of you,' he said. 'Why are you having this conversation with me and not the police?'

'Frankly, they're not interested now Elizabeth's home,' Tom said. 'They think she must have gone out with some friends and doesn't want to tell us about it. But she isn't like that and we know of at least one person out there who is after her.'

Simmonds nodded. 'I understand; however, it seems most unlikely that the cases are related.' He shook his head. 'I'm sorry I can't be of more help.'

Tom didn't want to leave. He also couldn't think what else to say, so in the end they thanked Simmonds for his time

151

and left. As they turned to walk back to the car, an early-evening mist entwined the beds and long grass, creating ghostly figures among the distant shadows.

Before they reached the gate, Tom stopped, then called back to him. 'Mr Simmonds, before we go, could I ask a favour?'

'What is it?'

'I don't suppose you're still in contact with Cassandra's parents?'

The men sat in silence for several miles as they drove home. The roads were narrow leading back to the motorway and Father Montague enjoyed watching the mist rise from the fields as the night drew in. He noticed for the first time how the sheep in the fields seemed indifferent to each other, failing to display the herd mentality of other animals. In the past, he had considered the biblical metaphor of the animals a little unfair on his parishioners. Watching another herd wandering in different directions, some chewing, others asleep, only strengthened that view.

'Can I ask you a question, Father? I'm sorry, did I wake you?' Tom laughed.

The priest smiled and shook his head. 'No, of course not. I was miles away. Ask away.' Given the length of time Tom had probably been dwelling on his question, he thought it unlikely he was about to be asked something straightforward. He was wrong.

'I'm sure you hear this a lot. It would help me to know the answer,' Tom continued. 'Why do you believe?'

Father Montague nodded. 'Tom, my answer always depends on who is asking,' he replied, 'and so for you it is very simple. Elizabeth.'

Tom took his eyes off the road to glance at him. 'What do you mean by that?'

'Each of us is guilty of taking for granted that which is most extraordinary,' Montague explained. 'But as a parent you have witnessed a miracle first-hand.'

Tom raised his eyes. 'I understand what you're saying. We both know the science involved. Eleventh-year biology explains that little miracle.'

'Science has shown us many truly wonderful things. It is yet to explain the human soul,' Montague said. 'It is all very well learning how something works – the magic lies in why it does.'

'Thanks for reminding me why you don't see me on a Sunday morning any more.'

Montague smiled. 'Then allow me a short sermon now,' he said. 'When you are moved by music or poetry or literature; or are struck with wonder standing before a masterpiece; or are consumed by awe, looking out across the slopes from the top of a mountain – these are all opportunities to see the world as greater than the sum of its parts.'

'That's just—' Tom started to reply before Montague cut him off.

'Permit me one further example, if I may, Tom,' he said. 'Let me take you back to that time in the hospital when you first looked into Elizabeth's dark-brown eyes. In that instant, you knew something miraculous had happened, despite understanding the science involved in giving her life. These moments are all around if we would only notice.'

Tom sighed and nodded. 'OK, you've passed the common entrance exam for parish priests,' he said. 'Well done.'

The men continued in silence for a time, winding through the villages until they reached the road to Brighton, connecting Lewes with the road back to London.

Montague thought about Elizabeth. He clearly remembered her baptism and how strands of her golden hair had darkened as he anointed her forehead with holy water. 'I baptise you in the name of the Father, the Son, and the Holy Spirit.' He had said those words so many times he rarely listened to them. So instead, that time he'd allowed his mind to wander and think about the baptism of Christ when the voice of the Lord had said, 'This is my own dear son with whom I am pleased.' No sooner had the thought crossed his mind than the clouds outside had parted and a brilliant ray of sunshine pierced the stained-glass window and washed over the head of the young girl. The timing was perfect and produced gasps, as well as smiles, from those in attendance.

During the car journey, Tom had enjoyed listening to his companion justify his faith and conceded that he had some interesting observations. Yet weren't they really arguments for the power of love and art? Or were those themselves reflections of God? He sniffed at the thought, and when Montague looked at him, he gestured with his head towards a passing motorist.

But the priest was right about one thing, he thought. His bond with his daughter was powerful and he would never allow someone to take her away from him.

Elizabeth was desperate to see Tobias. It was too risky to try going out at night again, so now she knew she must find another moment. That came one Saturday morning when her parents agreed that she could go to Freddie's house. She had no intention of visiting him, of course. Instead, she had seen the ferryman after school the evening before and asked him to take her across the next morning.

When she arrived at his hut the following day, Tobias was there. She told him the news about Maurice and how she had liked the school caretaker.

'He seemed so lonely,' she said. 'I hope he's at peace now.'

The boy looked away.

'What do you think happened to him, Tobias? When we saw him, he seemed fine. He must've gone into the river not long after we crossed.'

Her words hung in the evening air. Tobias didn't answer.

After crossing the river, they came to the woods and she saw a silver birch far wider than any she'd seen before. It was broad and tall and held its own among the oaks and pines.

'Tobias, look at this. Have you ever seen a tree like it?'

He seemed unmoved.

'It's so beautiful,' she continued. 'Shall we climb it?'

'Why would you want to do that?'

'Because it wants us to,' she replied, mesmerised by the light coming off the silvery bark that she imagined laid a path to the moon.

When he didn't reply, she stepped towards the tree and placed her palms on the smooth skin. Wrapping her arms around the trunk, she pressed her cheek against the papery bark. She imagined springing from bough to bough, forever upwards towards the stars. The woods smelt of warm straw. They walked under a canopy of young saplings that bowed their heads in a wedding arch over the path. Above them, the leaves were dappled in morning sunlight, and the birdsong was crisp and clear and joyous.

Elizabeth raised her arms and looked up. 'Isn't it wonderful in here, Tobias?' She completed a gentle pirouette and grinned.

'Why do you say that?'

She shook her head, still smiling.

'What do you see that's so wonderful?' he asked, confused.

She reached up and held one of the delicate light-green leaves between her thumb and forefinger. 'All of this, of course,' she replied. 'Nature.'

'It's just a tree.'

'Nothing is "just" anything,' she said. 'Perhaps if you look a little closer you might find something that surprises you.'

'Wise words from one so young.'

They turned to find the monk standing at the foot of a large fir tree. Its branches reached past the canopies of the other trees to the heavens.

'Life is indeed all about perspective,' he added. 'It's how we choose to look at things that gives them meaning. You should listen to her, boy: there is much she could teach you.'

'What are you doing here?' Tobias sounded nervous.

'I am never far away.' The monk turned to Elizabeth. 'A daytime visit today, I see?'

She moved closer to Tobias as the monk stepped away from the tree, blocking the path.

'You must take her back through the woods and let her return to her family,' he said to Tobias.

'This is nothing to do with you. She wants to come with me.'

'Actually, Tobias, I don't really care if we go to the house or not,' Elizabeth confessed. 'We could always explore the woods together a bit more.'

Tobias looked at the monk before motioning to Elizabeth to follow him back in the direction they had come from. As they walked, she asked why the monk had stopped them. Tobias told her it was because he thought she didn't belong there.

'Well, of course I don't belong here, but I can visit, can't I?'

'He doesn't think we should have any visitors,' Tobias said.

Elizabeth breathed deeply to take in the scent of the woods. She realised it had become colder the further they had gone along the path, and was warmer now they had retraced their steps. She heard the birds again and looked up at the row of saplings that trembled in the breeze.

Tom Fairchild woke up in the night. His head was still foggy from dreaming. He remembered no clear storyline aside from interactions with family members that were vivid and felt real. Many of them involved Elizabeth. He decided it was fuelled by his anxiety at nearly losing her. When he closed his eyes to get back to sleep, the bed sheets were wet with sweat. He rolled out of bed and returned from the bathroom with a towel. Before climbing back in, he went to check on Elizabeth. The door was closed, so he turned the handle carefully to avoid making any noise. He saw her outline under the duvet and went over to check. As he got closer he could see her body. He bent over to kiss her on the forehead and looked into the bluest eyes he'd ever seen. The boy smiled at him.

'Tom, what is it?' Mary woke suddenly on hearing him shout.

He was lying beside her and breathing heavily, beads of sweat on his brow. 'There's someone in Elizabeth's bed,' he replied, voice shaking.

'It was a dream, Tom. Everything's OK.'

He was sitting up now as she spoke to him. He jumped out of bed and ran into Elizabeth's room. He returned moments later and nodded at Mary, allowing himself a slight smile. When he pulled back the duvet to get into bed, he felt the towel his wife must have put there to stop his sweat spoiling the sheets. He lay on his side and watched her fall asleep.

The cry of gulls and the smell of sea air hit Tom as he left the car. The houses on the street were in poor condition and their pastel paint was cracked and flaking off the walls. The retired detective had told him that the family had moved to the coast when it became intolerable to stay where Cassandra had grown up. It took nearly five years for them to accept that she was never coming back.

When no one answered the door, a neighbour said Tom would find Cassandra's mother on the promenade. It was a short walk to the end of the street and over the road that ran alongside the front. The promenade was shared by pedestrians and cyclists, although it was largely deserted due to a cold, biting wind that threw sand into the faces of anyone brave enough to venture out. The first bench he saw was dedicated to the memory of a couple who had spent 'many happy times enjoying the view'. Sitting by the small metal plaque was an old woman clutching a brown handbag. She had long grey hair and her face was free of make-up.

'Mrs Porter?' He sat down next to her. 'Soothing, isn't it?'

'*The gentleness of heaven broods o'er the sea,*' she replied.

'Wordsworth?'

'My husband was an English teacher. I feel closer to them by the water.'

'Mrs Porter, my name's Tom Fairchild. DI Simmonds said you'd moved down here.'

'Do you have news?' she asked, looking at him.

He shook his head. 'I'm sorry, I don't. But I do need your help.'

Hope flickered across her eyes before disappearing like rain on the ocean. She turned back to the water and the horizon. 'I am no help to anyone, Mr Fairchild. I lost my daughter and couldn't save my husband.'

'Your husband?'

'With our baby now. The pain of being separated from her was too much for the poor man.'

Tom sat for a moment and tried to imagine losing a child, then a spouse. Momentarily, he was taken back to when he was a child at boarding school, remembering the dread of separation and the irrational fear of never seeing his parents again. He forced them out of his head. 'Well, I happen to think you can help me. And I believe if you do, it might help you too in some small way.'

She turned to him again.

'We live not far from where you did and have a daughter a similar age to Cassandra when she went missing,' he told her. 'Some nights ago, after we had gone to bed, she left the house to meet someone and didn't come back. We found her in the middle of the night by the river, upset and scared and refusing to tell us what had happened.'

Mrs Porter hung her head and he could see she was trying not to cry.

'I was hoping if I told you more about my daughter – and what's been happening – you might recognise something familiar.'

She took her hand from her face. 'Tom, you say?'

He nodded.

'I'm sorry, Tom. Your story brings back horrible memories but my Cassandra left us a very long time ago now. What happened to your daughter can't be related.'

They sat watching the waves until he broke the silence. 'Did Cassandra tell you about any new friends before she disappeared?'

The woman allowed herself the suggestion of a smile thinking about her daughter. 'She was such a sociable, happy child. She had so many friends.'

'Anyone she told you about that you hadn't met?'

Mrs Porter shook her head. 'No – we went through this so many times with Barry and his team. It was all school friends and a few children from the street who went to different schools.'

Tom hunched forward, resting his elbows on his knees, and watched the breakers throw spray onto the beach. Eventually he stood up and told Mrs Porter that he was deeply sorry for her loss. Walking back to his car, he heard the gulls call his name, before realising it was somebody shouting. Mrs Porter was now standing by the bench and waving. He ran back to her.

'There was a boy she used to talk about,' she said. 'We told the police about him. They said they were looking for a man.'

'What was his name?'

'I can't remember, it's been so long.'

He gave her time to think.

'It was unusual. You know, not Peter or John or anything like that.' Then she smiled and tears appeared at the corners of her eyes. '*To the valiant, actions speak alone.*'

'I'm sorry?' he asked.

'Smollett, the Scottish poet.'

Tom laughed and shook his head.

'He was a great favourite of my husband's, although I never cared much for him myself. That line does stick in the memory, though.'

'I should go. It was nice to meet you, Mrs Porter.'

'No, wait, Tom,' she said. 'Cassandra was seeing a boy with the same name as the poet. It was Tobias.'

THIRTEEN

The Missing Locket

With the death of the school caretaker, Simon Pankhurst found himself needing to counsel the children. They would seek him out after lessons to discuss what had happened and to try and make sense of events. They all wanted to know if he thought it was an accident or suicide. He told them he didn't know but suspected the poor man must have lost his footing and fallen into the river. One of the cleaners at the school said Maurice had never learned to swim, so he would have been powerless against the current that evening.

The weekends gave Pankhurst the opportunity to get away from school for a few hours and clear his head. Running gave him time to think, and on the Friday after Maurice Truman had been found dead, he changed into his running kit and set off for the river. Using the towpath on that particular stretch of the Thames involved negotiating lines of pushchairs, dog walkers and other runners, while keeping an eye out for cyclists. He enjoyed following the movement of the river with his eyes and matching his rhythm to its gentle pace. It was hypnotic and therapeutic, and as he established an easy breathing pattern, he started to sweat. The surface of the path was perilous with occasional potholes and he was careful to look down every few yards to make sure he didn't catch one. At dusk, the river would rise and cleanse the path, and as he ran, he saw that the residue of yesterday's high tide had left an undulating line of silt at its edge, next to the grass and vegetation on the bank. When he reached the lock, he returned the wave of a couple on a small pleasure boat as they waited for the water to rise between the gates. He had covered several miles and decided to turn back while he still had enough energy to repeat the distance. The sun was now in his face and he dipped his head slightly so that the peak of his cap shielded his eyes. The current had changed direction too and was now moving upstream, encouraging him along.

With his feet beating a steady tempo on the tarmac, he thought again about the school caretaker. The river seemed dirtier as it swelled and it was impossible to see the bed at its most shallow. At this time of year, Pankhurst knew it would be shockingly cold at night and he imagined the terror of falling into its swirling, suffocating grasp. He hoped it had been over quickly, although he found it hard to shake the idea of Truman suffering.

He took his eyes off the water to try and think of something else. His body felt good from the exercise, and before long he came to the next lock and the bridge to the town. As he went by, he turned his head to watch rowers at the boat club and a handful of early diners entering a riverside restaurant. He saw the ferry moored against its pontoon and continued on past a children's playground, towards the place where he had found Elizabeth after she'd become separated from the group on their outing.

Then he stopped running. Confused, he rested his hands on his hips to catch his breath. Precisely where Elizabeth had told him she had seen the ferryman, he now saw a large man in a rowing boat by the far bank. He could see from the pattern still on the water that the boat had crossed from the direction of the old ferryman's hut on Pankhurst's side of the river. The boat had now reached the far bank. When the rower stood up and reached out to steady his craft, Pankhurst realised there was someone else on board. The sun on the trees cast shadows across both the water and the small boat that rocked as its passenger disembarked. When she climbed the steps up the bank, a last ray caught the back of her head, illuminating her golden hair.

Pankhurst was so focused on the boat that he hadn't seen the priest approach. 'Hello, Father,' he said, surprised. 'Did you know there was still a ferry operating from here?' He raised his arm to point, then let it drop when he saw that the boat had gone. Sweat dripped off his head and nose and started to fall to the ground.

Father Montague looked across the water and shook his head. Two mallards came in to land with a splash and a clap of wings and pushed a small wave towards the bank with their flat orange feet. They chattered, hoping the two men had some bread for them.

'The ferry hasn't gone from here for many years,' Montague explained, clearing his throat. 'Well, before my time, in fact. As I'm sure you know, it moved further down the river where the pleasure boats are moored now and—'

Pankhurst cut him short. 'Yes, I am aware of that.' He thought about sharing what he had seen, then decided against it. He knew Father Montague had no more answers than he did. Instead, he wished him a good evening, explaining that he had to keep running as he was getting cold.

When he got home, he stretched on the doorstep. He pressed both hands against the door frame and pushed his heels into the ground, creating tension in the backs of his legs. He then held each shin in turn, pulling his heels into his buttocks, encouraging the tops of his thighs to flex against the pressure. When he felt he had broken up the acid in his muscles, he turned the key in the lock and stepped inside.

His home was an old almshouse, positioned in the middle of a row of identical cottages built centuries ago. He enjoyed the irony of their association with the poor and what he considered his own badly paid profession. He took the stairs two at a time and went into the bathroom. While he waited for the shower to get hot, he looked out of the window onto the garden, thinking again about what had happened. It had been close to a hundred yards away and he couldn't see who was rowing the boat. He had no doubt, though, about the passenger. He looked forward to asking her about it on Monday morning.

During assembly, Pankhurst noticed something remarkable. The sun came through the windows on the east side of the building, revealing tiny particles dancing in the light. He was at the back of the hall and watched it fall on Elizabeth's head and shoulders, two rows in front of him. Her hair seemed to come alive. Strands floated and shimmered in the rays and reflected a subtle array of glittering hues. He sat mesmerised until he realised he was being called to address the assembly. When he stood up, she turned and smiled at him.

Afterwards, he waited by the door for the assembly to end. Elizabeth was talking to Freddie Evans when Pankhurst reached out and took her arm.

'Elizabeth, can I have a word?'

She looked back at her companion and feigned horror, opening her mouth wide, before turning to go with Pankhurst. 'Is everything OK?' she asked, sounding more worried than she intended.

He waited until the rest of the children had filed out. Then he asked what she was doing crossing the river on her own on Saturday.

She had not been honest with him about the caretaker's disappearance, so decided the truth was actually her safest option this time. She admitted that she had taken the boat across the river to play with a friend. The harder question to answer was who had taken her across. 'I don't know his name but you always see him on the river,' she said. 'He doesn't say much, Mr Pankhurst. I'm sure he's quite harmless. All he likes doing is going back and forth across the river.' She tried a smile.

The teacher's mouth was open, then he shook his head.

'The first time I spoke to him, my father was there,' she continued, neglecting to clarify that the man had actually left by the time Tom arrived.

'So your father is happy for you to go out on the river with a man whose name you don't even know?'

She nodded.

'Is everything all right?' It was the head teacher.

Pankhurst was annoyed with Elizabeth, but wanted to find out what was really going on himself. He told the head that everything was fine and that he was just reminding

Elizabeth of the dangers of playing by the river after school, particularly in the light of what had happened to Mr Truman. The head teacher nodded and carried on down the stone steps from the assembly hall.

Elizabeth saw her chance and walked with her. 'Mrs Cuthbertson? I have a question about today's reading.'

Pankhurst bit his lip in irritation. 'Elizabeth, I'll see you later,' he called after her.

When she was small, Elizabeth had been given a gold locket by her grandmother that everyone said was irreplaceable. For that reason, she was told to wait until she started secondary school before wearing it and then only on special occasions. When her grandmother passed away, Elizabeth had secretly started putting it on as a way of staying close to her. Every night before she went to bed, she would clasp the jewellery in her hands, close her eyes, and tell her grandmother what had happened that day and how much she loved her.

That weekend, after returning from the river, she arrived home before her parents. In her room, she reached instinctively for the locket. When it wasn't there, she felt the pain of bereavement all over again. Her mind raced as she played back the day's events. She remembered hugging the silver birch before they saw the monk and wondered if it was then that one of the delicate links in the necklace's fine chain had given way. Tears pooled in her eyes. There were no excuses for losing it – she wasn't meant to be wearing it. Her parents would blame her despite what she considered mitigating circumstances. The more she thought about it, the less inclined she felt to tell them. They would never forgive her for going to the river again. She lay down on the bed and cried when she realised that there was only one thing for it. She would have to return to the woods and find it.

At school the next week, it was all she could think about. She was deep in thought by one of the apple trees at the end of the playground when someone jumped out from behind it.

'Jesus Christ! What do you think you're playing at? You scared me half to death.'

The boy went red and looked at the ground. 'Sorry,' he muttered, then sniggered.

'It's not funny. You frightened me.'

'I was just trying to get your attention. You've been away with the fairies all day.'

She frowned. 'Well, that's my prerogative, isn't it?'

'I don't know,' he replied.

'What?' she shouted. She liked Freddie Evans but he'd picked the wrong time to play the fool.

'I don't know what "prerogative" means,' he explained, struggling to repeat the word and looking embarrassed.

They stared at each other, unsure where the conversation should go from here. She was still cross with him and narrowed her mouth to show it. Freddie took the opportunity to do what he did best. He imitated her. She knew a game of poker face was futile against him and rolled her eyes. He crossed his eyes and tried to touch the end of his nose with his tongue. She shook her head and laughed.

'There, doesn't that feel better?' he asked.

'You know, Freddie, sometimes people like to be left alone with their thoughts.'

'Only the unhappy ones,' he replied, 'and you don't want to be one of those.'

They started walking together past an apple tree.

'A problem shared is a problem spared, you know.'

'Really, and who told you that?' she asked.

'I don't remember. I've heard grown-ups say it.'

She shrugged. 'Well, I've never heard it before.'

'You've heard them say "prerogative", though,' he said, failing again to pronounce it properly.

They walked down the gravel path separating the playground from the lawn, until they arrived at the rear entrance to the school. She thought about confiding in him. The boy from the house had said that it must remain a secret and she should tell no one. But she had to retrieve her grandmother's locket and she had a feeling she was going to need help to do it.

'If I tell you a secret, Freddie, can you promise not to tell another soul?'

'I promise.'

'I mean it, Freddie. If you break your promise, I'll never talk to you again. That's my promise.'

'Cross my heart and hope to die.'

She thought for a moment how best to tell him. 'I've lost something very valuable, and if my parents find out, my life won't be worth living.'

'That sounds a bit harsh.' He sniggered, quickly stopping when he saw she was serious. 'What's missing?'

She told him about the locket and how her grandmother had given it to her shortly before she died. He offered to help find it.

That night, she dreamed again of Tobias. She was looking for her locket and he wouldn't help. When she asked him why not, she suddenly found herself talking with her grandmother, who told her to stop searching and just remember her instead.

She woke up with a start and looked at the clock. It was still night-time. She felt hot, and got up to draw back the curtain and open the window. The cool air hit her face as she watched the thin branches on the nearest tree tremble in the breeze. The moon glowed against the black sky and warmed the edge of a bank of clouds that rose to engulf the gold crescent.

The next day, she told Freddie about the dream. He wondered if it meant that she knew the locket couldn't bring her grandmother back.

'So you're not going to help me look for it?'

'That's not what I said.'

'You know how much it means to me, Freddie. I haven't told anyone else about it.'

'When do you want to look, then?' he asked.

'Friday.'

'After school?'

'No, later than that. I don't know how long it's going to take.' She watched him look at the floor. 'Scared?'

'No! Don't be stupid,' he muttered.

'I'll meet you by the old ferryman's shed at midnight, then. The one I showed you when we went down there with the class.'

'Midnight?! Elizabeth, are you mad? I can't be out that late. And how will you find it in the dark?'

'With a torch, of course. I'll go on my own, then.' She

paused for effect. 'I'm surprised you'd let a girl go out into the woods on her own in the middle of the night.'

'You don't have to go,' he said. 'Your grandmother said you didn't.'

She rolled her eyes and started to walk off.

He ran after her. 'Why do we have to go so late?'

'Because we need to cross the river when no one else is about. Pan saw me last time.'

'Do your parents know about this?'

'Of course they don't know about it, Freddie, that's the whole point.'

'So who's taking us across?'

'The ferryman.'

'Seriously, Elizabeth.'

'He works on special occasions, taking people across the river. I can't tell you any more than that.'

'Why not?'

'Because it's a secret.'

'OK, this is too weird for me. You should definitely tell your parents about this.'

'You promised me, Freddie.'

'I know I did. I won't say anything,' he said, 'but I really think you should. You didn't mean to lose the locket. It was an accident.'

'OK, if you won't come, then at least cover for me.'

'What do you mean?'

'Come to mine after school today. Then ask me – in front of my parents – if I can come to yours for tea and a sleepover on Friday.'

'Why do you want to do that?'

She sighed and rolled her eyes. 'I don't want to, Freddie.

171

I'll come for tea, but you're giving me an alibi so I can go and look for my locket that night.'

He looked confused.

'An alibi. You know, a cover story?'

The penny dropped and Freddie agreed to the plan.

Freddie Evans was standing at his living-room window, waiting for Elizabeth to arrive. They had arranged to meet at 5pm and he was keen to see her the moment she appeared. Fifteen minutes before their rendezvous, he caught sight of a thin blonde girl in her school uniform and told his mother that she was here. He then rushed out of the house and across the front lawn to meet her.

When he reached the front gate, she wasn't there. Stepping out onto the pavement, he saw her heading towards the churchyard and called out. She didn't stop. When he got to the church, she was standing by a yew tree that cast its protective boughs over a chest tomb hosting a long-deceased local dignitary.

'Why didn't you stop?'

She had her back to him, appearing to read the inscription on the grave.

'Elizabeth? What are you doing?'

When she turned around, Freddie froze.

'Oh, I'm sorry, I thought you were someone else,' he stammered.

'Who were you looking for?' the girl asked.

'My friend, Elizabeth. We were meant to be meeting.'

'You can't save her.'

'I'm sorry, what?! Who are you?' Freddie asked, his voice breaking.

'My name is Sandra,' she said, before turning away and walking through the churchyard towards the river.

Freddie watched her go and then ran back home. When he got there, Elizabeth was at the front door talking to his mother, who was looking worried.

'Elizabeth!' he exclaimed. 'Thank heavens.' When he saw that they were confused, he held up his hands. 'I'm sorry,' he added. 'I can explain.'

At the end of the week, Simon Pankhurst acted on a hunch. The Friday before, he had seen Elizabeth crossing the river, so he decided to see if she would do it again today. As soon as school finished, he made his way down to the riverbank where she must have crossed. He then walked up the towpath until he reached the first large trees and overgrowth that afforded some cover from where he could watch unobserved. Then he waited.

He had brought a book for company, pausing between pages to glance back along the water to where he expected to see her. Several hours passed, and he watched various pleasure craft and paddleboarders enjoying the water, as well as assorted river fowl that patrolled tirelessly, looking for morsels of food. Before long, the light started to go from the day and the number of people using the towpath dropped to the occasional dog walker or cyclist coming home from work. He was no longer able to read his book, so he put it in his backpack and finished the last of his flask. He decided to give it another twenty minutes.

It was at the exact moment he broke cover to head home that he saw her. Even in the low light, her hair was unmistakable. He didn't call out because he wanted to find out who she was meeting. Careful not to be seen, he stepped away from the riverbank and moved slowly alongside the bowed stone wall that ran alongside the towpath to where she was standing. Checking to see if anyone else was coming along the path, he increased his pace before reaching out to put his hand on her shoulder. As he did, she stepped forward, eluding his grasp, and slipped feet first into the water.

'Elizabeth, no!' He fell to his knees and reached down for her. He couldn't feel her body under the water and it was too dark to see anything. He shouted for her again and jumped into the river, feeling his feet hit the soft bed before slipping and taking him under. He forced his way to the surface and called for help.

The lights from a vehicle swung across the water and his waving arms and shouts caught the attention of the driver, who parked close to the edge and scrambled down the bank to pull Pankhurst out. After he'd explained what had happened, they used the narrow beam of the headlights to search for Elizabeth in the water. A woman walking a dog stopped to ask if she could help and offered to call the emergency services.

The wall by the footpath turned blue when the police arrived and the officers spread out along the bank to look for signs of life. Soon, an ambulance pulled up and two paramedics wrapped the teacher in a blanket before moving him into the back of the vehicle to assess his injuries. When they told him he would be all right, he burst into tears. He told them how he'd tried to save her before she just disappeared.

Later that evening, Pankhurst was on the phone telling his sister what had happened when he saw an incoming call from an unknown number. He told her he'd ring her straight back and then walked over to look out the window while he took the call. He feared the worst, and after confirming his name and listening to what the police officer had to say, the mobile slipped from his hand to the floor and he stumbled backwards against the edge of the sofa. He steadied himself before picking up the phone again.

'Mr Pankhurst? Are you still here? Hello?'

'Yes, I'm sorry, I dropped the phone,' he muttered. 'Please say that again; I don't understand.'

The policewoman repeated what she had told him and he began to cry for the second time that night.

FOURTEEN

The Octagon

Tobias wasn't there this time when the ferryman took her across. After leaving the woods, she approached the grounds of the house. Walking alongside an ornamental hedge at the rear of the property, she came to a tiny fairy-tale woodland garden. Dipping her head to avoid the overhanging climbers, she followed the soft green path the gardener had cut into the lawn, until she arrived at one of several summer houses.

They were bigger inside than they appeared, with hard wooden seating that followed the semicircular shape of the outer wall. On either side was an opening. Usually Elizabeth would dart inside with Tobias and they would pull their feet up onto the seat and hug their knees. It was their favourite place to regroup and plan before heading into the house. So which summer house was he in? She decided upon one of the small shelters painted a faded duck-egg-blue colour, so was surprised to find it empty. She thought about calling his name but decided to keep looking.

She carried on along the path that curved through a wedge of tall, thin-stemmed plants that bowed in the breeze as she went past. The next summer house looked brand new and was painted a brilliant red. As she approached, she detected movement and stopped. Something had caught her eye. It made no sound. She crouched down so no one would be able to see her from the window and crept closer.

'It's all right, child, I know you're there.'

She stood up slowly to look through the window. The summer house was empty. She looked over her shoulder to make sure he wasn't creeping up behind her. No one was there. Her eyes darted from left to right as she planned her escape route.

'Please come inside and talk with me,' he said.

'Who is it?' Elizabeth's voice trembled. 'I didn't see anyone inside.'

He laughed and she thought she recognised his voice. 'You're looking in the wrong one.'

She turned to her right and saw another shelter with an old crucifix hanging on the outside. She wondered to herself if this place was magical.

The monk she had seen in the woods dipped his head as he emerged from his hiding place. 'There is magic all around us if we only know where to look,' he explained.

Although she was afraid of him, she thought his eyes looked kind when he smiled at her. 'I don't understand.'

'The moon above us controls the tides and slows our world. It also guides you tonight. People forget to look up. There is more to see than they realise,' he replied.

'That's not quite what I meant,' she said. 'I was talking about the summer houses.'

The monk shook his head. 'These huts have unusual acoustics, that is all,' he replied, waving his arm dismissively.

'Please, come inside where we can talk,' he said, motioning towards the one he had been sitting in.

'I'd prefer to stay here.'

'There comes a time in your life when you have to trust someone new for the first time,' he said. 'The people in the house do not have your best interests at heart. You know that, which is why you're meeting the boy down here and why you didn't want to risk being discovered by calling out for him. What I have to say to you cannot be said out in the open; we need to be careful.'

'I will come in only if you move to the other side and allow me to sit just inside this entrance,' she said.

He moved to the far side of the semicircular bench and went down on his knees. 'Why are you here?' he asked.

'I'm meeting Tobias.'

'You should be at home with your family. Instead, you cross the river and come to a place that holds real danger for you. You can feel it. So I ask you again: why are you here?'

She sat in silence and thought about the question. 'I like Tobias, and it's exciting going to the house and making sure no one sees us,' she explained. 'I want him to help find my locket. And I don't think it's really dangerous or I wouldn't come. They just have parties we haven't been invited to, that's all.'

The monk sat up straight and lifted his face to the heavens. 'On the contrary, child, their party is one that you, above all, others are invited to,' he said. 'It is a gathering in your honour.'

She looked confused.

'People believe in many things,' he explained, slowly shaking his head. 'But what their gods all have in common is that they offer hope of salvation. Has the boy told you of the book?'

Elizabeth nodded.

'The book is of no concern to you.' Tobias stood in the doorway.

'That is not true. It was stolen from me.'

The boy gestured to her with his head to leave.

'Child, you are not the first to come to this house seduced by the promise of adventure and friendship. Each time you come, your chances of leaving diminish greatly.'

Elizabeth looked at Tobias. When he didn't reply, she turned back to see the monk leaving.

'Come on, let's get out of here,' Tobias suggested.

She got up and stepped down out of the summer house onto the grass. 'Why's he leaving?' she asked.

'Who cares?' the boy replied. 'Probably in search of some other children to frighten.'

Elizabeth smiled and followed him back along the long hedge at the perimeter of the garden. She admired his bravery in the face of such intimidating men as the ferryman and the monk, and yet there was something at the back of her mind that bothered her. Despite Tobias dismissing him, the monk had seemed sincere, and there was one thing in particular he'd said that unsettled her. Was it true there had been other children who had visited the house like her? And if there had, what had happened to them? As they walked, she played over in her mind the conversation. Had Tobias brought other friends across the river to the party? And also, why hadn't he been there to make the crossing with her tonight? That had never happened before.

'I know what you're thinking.' He had stopped alongside the kitchen garden, where a latticework of canes would support the summer's runner beans.

'You do?'

'I'm sorry for not meeting you at the river. I was needed elsewhere. I knew you'd find me.'

Was he deliberately ignoring what the monk had said or had he not realised the effect it had on her?

'And as for what the monk said when we left,' he continued, 'he's wrong. You're the only person I've invited to the house. That should be obvious from how happy my aunt was that I'd finally found a friend.'

Elizabeth thought back to when she'd met Gabriella and it was true that she had seemed delighted that her nephew had a companion. Then why would the monk lie to her, unless he was simply trying to scare her away? '*Was* the book taken from him?' Her words hung in the night air. 'Tobias?'

The pair continued walking as if nothing had been said.

'Why are you ignoring me?'

'Why don't you ask him yourself?' he replied.

'He already told me—' Elizabeth began.

'Not the monk,' Tobias interrupted. 'Solomon. The librarian. Come on, I'll take you to him.'

As they walked, Tobias was more interested in telling her about the book than hearing about her missing locket.

'If you don't believe me, I can show you what it says about you,' he said, as they passed a spider's web with a tiny insect crystallised against one of the silver strands.

'I think I'll pass if it's all the same to you,' she said, not wanting to be chased again.

He went to say something, then turned away.

'What is it?' she asked. 'Tell me, Tobias.'

'You won't find your locket, then,' he said quietly.

'What did you say?!'

'Your locket. It isn't here. They have it.'

'How did they know it was mine? Did you tell them?' Her voice rose in pitch.

He hung his head. 'I had no choice. They made me. They'll do anything to see you.'

She felt herself back in the maze. 'How about you? What's your role in all of this?' she asked him. 'If I'm the prize catch, you must be the bait.'

His bottom lip started to tremble. 'I'm sorry,' he said. 'I'm only doing what I was told. They promised they won't hurt you.'

She knew she must think quickly. Leaving now without the locket meant she would most likely never get it back.

'That's not true.'

The voice made her jump and goosebumps danced up the back of her neck. The monk must have taken a shortcut to get ahead of them.

'What's not true?' she asked, a note of hysteria entering her voice.

'If you go with the boy, they most certainly will hurt you,' he said. 'Remember how they chased you last time? And now they have tricked you. That is not the behaviour of those who mean you no harm.'

'Don't listen to him, Elizabeth,' Tobias urged, moving closer to her. 'I told you the truth about the book. Let me show you what it says and then you'll believe me.'

'And no doubt those lunatics from the house will be

waiting to tell me all about it too,' Elizabeth replied, starting to panic.

'You are right to be suspicious, child,' the monk said. 'You must forget the locket and go home while you can.'

She didn't understand why Tobias had lied to her and wanted to believe him. The monk scared her and if she left to go home, he might follow her. There was no way she was doing that. 'Tobias, if I come with you,' she said, 'I want you to promise me two things. You'll help me get my grandmother's locket back, and you have to protect me and make sure the others don't find us.'

The monk moved closer. 'If you go to them now, I cannot save you. They will never let you leave.'

She turned again when Tobias spoke. Two simple words that sounded like the sweetest notes of a nightingale's song on this coldest of nights.

'I promise,' the boy said.

With her decision made, Edmund turned and walked away, his angular body cutting through the descending gloom like a sail on a still night. She felt tired and realised how badly prepared she was to be outside for so long. Her only warm clothing was a cream woollen cardigan that she wore over a red dress and white leggings. Despite the start of spring, she wished she was wearing a thick coat, scarf and hat to keep warm. Her teeth chattered and she lifted her shoulders to try and retain the heat she was losing around her neck. Tobias was equally ill-dressed for the cool weather, in a long-sleeved white shirt and dark trousers. Despite this, he showed no sign of discomfort.

'Tobias, I'm cold. Is there somewhere we can go to warm up?'

He nodded. 'There will be a fire where they're keeping the locket.'

Soon the ground in front of them was higher and they stood outside an octagon-shaped building that looked like a large castle turret.

'What is this place, Tobias?'

'It used to be a monastery,' he said. When she looked confused, he added, 'All that's left is the chapter house.'

She was surprised to discover the remains of a monastery close to her home. 'Is this why the monk is here?'

'Probably.'

'What happened to the other monks?'

'What do you mean?'

'Well, where did they go? And what about the other buildings?' She had so many questions. 'And why did the chapter house survive?'

'That one's easy,' he said. 'The monks had a library full of the most important books in the world. They met in the chapter house to discuss the most valuable ones.'

'Are the books still there?'

'One of them is,' he said and smiled. 'I'll show you. It's the missing one you asked about before and they're probably keeping your locket in the chapter house too.'

'Why bring it here?' she asked as they walked up to the building. 'Or is it some sort of military fort where they keep stolen jewellery safe from rampaging girls who want it back?' She laughed.

'No one stole the locket from you, Elizabeth. You lost it, remember?'

The door of the building had rusted iron studs and hinges cut into the faded, splintered wood.

'There won't be anyone in here, will there, Tobias?' she asked nervously, reaching for the metal ring that served as a door handle.

'No, don't,' he instructed. 'Let's look through one of the windows first.'

They crept along the outside wall to the nearest one, which was the height of two men and arch-shaped, with many panes of glass divided into squares. At the top, the sides were curved. The broad windowsill allowed them to reach up and peer inside. As the last of the sun's rays illuminated the inside through the stained glass, she thought the room looked beautiful. Like a church, the Octagon had wooden panelling on the walls and an almost orange parquet floor that fanned inwards to the centre of the room, where there was a high table made of veined marble. They squatted outside, peering in for a final time to make sure no one was inside.

'I think I can see it!' she exclaimed. 'Look, Tobias, you can just make out the chain hanging off the far side of that table.'

'That's not a table.'

'What do you mean?'

'It's an altar.'

The door was heavy and difficult to open, despite Elizabeth putting her entire weight behind it. Inside, the chapter house was larger than it appeared from the outside. Closing the door sealed the chamber. The room felt like a place of worship, with its high ceiling and immaculate silence. Their eyes were drawn to the altar in the middle of the floor, but when she walked over to it, the chain wasn't there.

'Where's my locket, Tobias?'

'I thought it would be here.'

'Why?'

'I saw Solomon heading this way from the house one day and wanted to see what he was doing, so I followed him. It would be here if he had it.'

'How do you know that?'

'I'll show you.'

He approached the lectern next to the altar and turned to Elizabeth. She saw a large book in front of him opened in the middle and walked over to get a better look.

'Is this the one from the library?'

'Solomon's pride and joy,' Tobias said. 'He is certain it can foresee what is to come.'

Her eyes widened. 'So he knows everything that's going to happen?'

Tobias shook his head. 'Not quite.' He told her that the book listed a specific sequence of events, which Solomon believed made it as important as the Bible. Tobias found it too hard to read, so they sat cross-legged on the floor while he told her what it meant.

'So why is this the only book left in this building?' she asked.

'Would you like me to answer that?'

They turned and jumped to their feet.

'Well?' Solomon asked.

Elizabeth looked at Tobias, who remained expressionless, so she nodded at Solomon.

'The chapter house is its spiritual home,' he explained. 'The book was studied here for many years by the monks and it is the only volume that deserves contemplation in such splendid isolation.'

Elizabeth remembered her question from earlier. 'Why did the monks leave?'

Solomon looked uncomfortable and glanced at Tobias before answering. 'All good things come to an end,' he replied, trying to smile, 'and they were kind enough to leave some reading for inquisitive minds to enjoy.'

While he was talking, Tobias had edged around the room towards the door. She didn't think Solomon had noticed, but then the librarian stuck out a leg to block Tobias's escape route.

'Where are you going, boy?' he said and bent down to look Tobias in the eye. 'Don't you know it's rude to leave without saying goodbye? And what about your friend here – surely you weren't going to leave her all alone with me?' He smiled.

Tobias moved back next to her in the centre of the room. He whispered something in her ear and then walked across to the perimeter of the room again. As he did, Solomon moved in parallel, like a dancer in step with his partner. At that moment, Elizabeth bolted for the door as Tobias had instructed. Her movement caught Solomon's attention, and when he looked across at her, Tobias ran past him on the other side. They both vaulted the steps down from the building to the lawn outside, with Tobias laughing as he flew through the air. Elizabeth stumbled as she hit the ground, then regained her footing and stayed close to him. She heard the old man shouting from inside the chapter house. She knew he couldn't catch them. She felt too scared to breathe but was still thrilled by what had happened. They retraced their steps away from the Octagon and back into the woods, pausing to check that he wasn't following them, before laughing as they set off again. When it was safe to walk, Tobias told her he was happy that she had seen the book.

'Why did he try to stop us leaving?' she asked. 'And what about my locket, Tobias? You said you'd help me find it!'

'I will. Solomon must have it. He's very protective of the book and considers the Octagon his private place.' He looked at her and smiled. 'Don't worry about him; he can't do anything. Come on, I'll take you back to the river. Your locket will turn up.'

Earlier that evening, Pankhurst was at his kitchen table nursing a glass of whisky when there was a knock at the door. He wasn't expecting anyone and it made him jump. He stood up carefully and walked through the living room to answer it.

'Simon, may I come in?'

'Tom! Is everything OK? I'm so sorry, I don't know what happened earlier,' Pankhurst replied, motioning for him to come through to the kitchen.

Tom pulled out a chair and sat down. He looked at the bottle of single malt on the table and then at the teacher, who gave an embarrassed smile and shrugged, saying it was Friday night after all. He then asked if Tom wanted one.

Tom laughed. 'Sure, why not?' he said. 'So what happened tonight, then?'

Pankhurst poured him a drink and asked if he wanted ice. He decided to leave out the part about him lying in wait for Elizabeth. 'I had been for a walk by the river after school,' he began, 'and was on my way back when I thought I saw

Elizabeth by the water's edge. When I went over to speak to her, she slipped and I couldn't reach her, so I jumped in to try and pull her out.'

'But you didn't see her, did you?'

Pankhurst saw Tom glance at the whisky bottle. 'Look, I know what you're thinking. I hadn't been drinking! I haven't had a drop all week, until tonight,' he added.

Tom nodded. 'Well, I can tell you this: Mary was very upset to take a call from the police tonight asking if Elizabeth was at home. Particularly as Elizabeth was having tea at Freddie's house at the time.'

'Tom, this girl was her spitting image,' Pankhurst protested. 'And I know the police said they couldn't find anything so she must have drowned.'

'Did she say anything to you?'

'No, she didn't even look at me. Why?'

Tom slowly turned the crystal tumbler in his hand. 'There was something strange that happened tonight,' he said. 'I mentioned Elizabeth had arranged to meet Freddie after school, but his mother told Mary he wasn't there when she called for him.'

'He's not missing, is he?' Pankhurst asked.

'No, he's not. He came home just after Elizabeth arrived. He had left the house because he thought he saw her walk past outside.'

The teacher motioned for him to continue.

'Freddie followed the girl he had seen to the churchyard, where she told him her name was Sandra, or at least that's what he thought she said. He then said she headed off in the direction of the river.'

'Where I saw her...' Pankhurst added.

'I think I need another drink,' Tom said, pushing his glass across the table.

*

A week had passed and Elizabeth still hadn't recovered her locket. She decided she would have to search for it alone without Tobias. She slipped out of the house in the early hours. It was a cold, clear night and the moon sat like a goose egg on the tops of the trees. She felt its pull as she watched the reflection light up the small sailing boats rocking by the bank. Light danced off the tiny waves that divided the familiar from what lay ahead. The river was the bridge between two worlds. She stood at the water's edge and could make out the house between the trees for the first time. Light from two windows upstairs illuminated the facade, framed by the leafless branches of two dead trees either side of it.

She made the crossing again on her own with the ferryman, then headed along the towpath towards the woods. The moon seemed to grow larger, helping her see her way and protecting her, she thought. When she approached a familiar tree ahead, it appeared to have aged a hundred years since the last time she saw it. Its leaves were pale in the moonlight and its low boughs stretched outwards like tentacles ready to pick her up.

It was then that she had the feeling of being watched. On one of the boughs that pointed towards the river was a sentry. The crow's head twitched when it was spotted. Child and scavenger stared at each other. It was the first time she had seen a bird at night other than an owl and the crow was as alert as if it were the middle of the day. She raised her arms and clapped. Instead of flying off, it dropped onto the path a few feet away. It occurred to her that it might be a lost pet and she suddenly felt guilty. She crouched down and put her hand out. The crow flew up and brought its talons towards her face. Before she could react, there was a blur of movement to her right and an animal took the bird in its mouth. The creature shook its head violently from side to side and leapt over the stone wall by the path. Elizabeth fell backwards and sat on the ground, looking at a puff of small grey feathers floating back to earth in front of her. She felt grit pressing painfully into the palms of her hands.

'This is not the first time I have told you it is not safe here at night.'

The monk approached her from the other side of the tree with a gesture similar to the one she had made to the bird. She imagined the same animal exploding out of the bushes and snatching her in its jaws. The thought was more terrifying than the monk, so she went towards him.

'What was that?' she asked.

'The fox was hungry.'

'Why did the crow attack me?'

'The woods at night do strange things to those living here,' he said. 'Come, we should move on.'

They walked along the path until he sat down on the trunk of a fallen tree and motioned for her to join him. She pulled herself up using the stub of a broken branch, careful to remain out of reach.

'Why have you come back?' he asked.

She reminded him about the missing jewellery and why she had to find it.

'The people from the house took it so that you would return.'

She told him he was wrong and that she had lost it in the woods. 'Who are you, anyway, and what are you doing out here?' she asked.

The hood of his cloak hid his eyes and he spoke as if in the confessional. 'My name is Edmund. I am the only one who can save you.' He lifted his head and watched her closely. 'We are all on a journey,' he said. 'Some know where they are going; others do not. Then there are those who are so lost, they don't even know it.'

Elizabeth thought for a moment. 'Like the people in the house?'

He nodded.

'What about you?' she said.

A scream penetrated the woods, making her flinch, and the fine hairs on her arms stood on end.

'Our friend is still hungry,' Edmund said.

She imagined blood on the white frill of the hunter's mouth and shut her eyes, trying to control a panic that threatened to overwhelm her. 'I'm scared,' she said, but he had left.

*

'You know, Tom, there's something that's been bothering me.'

Tom watched Father Montague pull up a stool at the bar. 'Good evening to you too, Father.'

The priest laughed. 'I'm sorry, I've been a little preoccupied. I was hoping I'd catch you here.'

Tom bought him a drink. 'What's on your mind?'

Montague nodded before taking a mouthful of beer. He wiped his mouth with the back of his hand and leant forward. Although it was still early, he didn't want the few customers in the pub to overhear. 'This might sound crazy; however, I do think there might be a pattern to Elizabeth's disappearances.'

'I don't see one. It's happened three times and several months apart. The only pattern is that it's out of character and she won't tell me who she's meeting.'

Montague reached for his drink again. He knew this was not going to be easy. 'When we went to look for her, it was March 18th, which was a Friday. And that was the third time it happened, right?'

Tom nodded.

'And the second time was October 20th, on a Wednesday, if I remember correctly. Didn't you say the first time she wandered off was around the harvest festival?'

'I've no idea when the harvest festival is,' Tom snapped. 'We found her down by the river for the first time on Monday, September 20th. She had just gone back to school after the summer holidays.'

'September 20th,' Montague repeated. He took his phone out of his pocket.

'Phone a friend, is it?' Tom took another mouthful of beer.

The priest turned on his stool and showed him the screen.

'What am I looking at?'

'It was a full moon, Tom,' Montague replied, showing him a lunar calendar.

'Are you serious?'

Montague pointed out the window at the moon that cast its milky light on the dark river running by the pub. 'Still bright, Tom, although not as full as it was the week before we went to visit Barry Simmonds. Or indeed the day after the harvest festival.'

Tom looked at him. 'It's a coincidence. And even if it's not, so what?'

'That I can't answer. If it's not a coincidence, then it stands to reason you need to be extra vigilant whenever a full moon approaches.'

Tom ordered another beer. He waited for it to arrive before speaking again. 'So you're suggesting my daughter is being pursued by a lunar-worshipping cult?' He had raised his voice, so that a couple at the corner table looked over.

Montague shuffled his stool closer and placed his hand on Tom's arm. 'I'm not the enemy here, you know that.'

'Those that are do sound a little far-fetched, don't you think?'

Montague took a mouthful of beer and smiled. 'I haven't the faintest idea what's going on here either. What I do think is, it's notable that each of these episodes has occurred during a full moon. There are some strange people out there,' he added.

'Well, if you're right then we won't have long to wait for them to try again.'

Montague nodded. 'Just another three weeks,' he said.

After a pause, Tom spoke again. 'There were full moons between these events and nothing happened,' he said. 'However, if your theory is correct, no pagan fruitcake would miss the opportunity to celebrate a super blood moon with the blood of a virgin.'

The priest winced and left the remainder of his beer, adding that he hoped to see Tom at church in the morning.

Tom knew it was unfair to take out his frustration on Father Montague, which made him wonder if his overreaction was because there was an outside chance he could be right. These were no ordinary circumstances, so there was likely no simple explanation for Elizabeth's behaviour. Tom hadn't noticed the timing with the full moons and it made him consider the implications of September's moon. He knew that there were cultures who worshipped lunar cycles, though the idea of someone sharing their beliefs being behind his daughter's abduction seemed absurd. But Montague was right about the timing.

Tom drained the last of his beer and pushed the glass across the bar. When he left the pub, he stopped to watch the moon playing hide-and-seek behind the clouds. Elizabeth had always loved it, so perhaps that was the connection. That made more sense. But then why had her behaviour not occurred in other months? Perhaps she'd lacked the opportunity, he thought. Or perhaps she was only subconsciously aware of where the moon was in its cycle. That was unlikely. *So the moon plays its part in this mystery. But for whom? Maybe both parties.* Either way, he was beginning to think that the supermoon was not only significant but portentous, and would bring a denouement to this strange time in their lives. Finally, he felt ahead of events and in a position to prevent Elizabeth falling into any more danger. It made sense that she would choose a specific lunar phase to leave the house, but he wanted to coax it out of her.

He held the handrail as he went down the steps from the pub to the pavement, and then stepped out into the empty road. The tide was out and the river coursed by on its journey to the sea. The moonlight flashed like Morse code on the crests of the tiny waves. It told of the secrets of the night, if he could only decipher them.

As he walked back to the vicarage, Father Montague thought about what Tom had said about the lunar eclipse. It had given him pause and he was unsure why.

When he was midway through the churchyard, the penny dropped. It was a line from Scripture: Joel 2:31. He gave an involuntary shiver as the words played out in his mind.

The sun will be turned to darkness, and the moon to blood, before the great and dreadful day of the Lord comes.

FIFTEEN

Blood Moon

It was now May. With the eclipse around the corner, Tom suggested that Mary mention it once more in front of Elizabeth over breakfast. As it turned out, he needn't have bothered as it came up on the radio. They were getting the bowls and cereal out when the weather forecaster handed back to the breakfast show host, who asked about the lunar eclipse.

The meteorologist explained how the country was set to experience 'a spectacular natural event that happens only once in a generation', adding that 'in May, listeners may notice the moon looking particularly full as a result of passing closer than usual to the earth'. She said, 'What will make it extra special is it will cross the earth's shadow and appear blood red to anyone watching in the UK and across the Americas.'

'Excited, sweetheart?'

'What do you think, Dad?' Elizabeth smiled.

'Is there anyone else at school who loves the moon like you do, Elizabeth?' Mary asked innocently.

Elizabeth shrugged.

'I bet there's some brainy kid who could tell you the facts and figures around a blood moon,' Tom tried.

'*Super* blood moon, Dad,' Elizabeth corrected him. 'Mr Isaac will. But I've not heard any mention of it.'

Tom thought about her science teacher, then dismissed the idea that he was involved. Elizabeth had only given the name of a boy, and if Isaac was involved, he didn't need to see her after school. 'How do you get on with him anyway?'

Elizabeth rolled her eyes and snored.

Mary laughed and gave her a kiss. 'OK, enough of this chit-chat,' she said. 'We all need to get upstairs and get dressed or we'll be late this morning.'

Elizabeth left the table and went with her, while Tom stirred what was left of his tea and studied the milky brown whirlpool for answers. Elizabeth would either make a champion poker player, or she was telling the truth and this time the moon had no deeper meaning for her. In that case, it was either a coincidence (which he now didn't believe) or it did in fact mean something to someone else. Whoever it was, they were not at her school.

That evening, Tom was on the sofa resting his legs on a footstool he had just stood on to reach a volume on selenology from the top of the bookcase. He was revisiting the lunar eclipse of 1982, familiarising himself with how it had coincided with flooding and chaos as rivers burst their banks, damaging homes and properties and closing roads. People had complained of being unable to sleep due to the bright nights or perhaps the satellite's closer orbit to earth had exerted a gravitational pull on their very souls. He remembered clearly the super blood moon when he was at school, but wasn't sure exactly why December of that year seemed to have added significance.

The television was on and Elizabeth sat beside him with her head against his chest. She had helped Mary tidy away the plates after dinner and was allowed to stay up late tonight to watch a programme about the eclipse. The presenter said it wouldn't be visible until around 2.30am on Monday, when a veil would be drawn slowly across the face of the moon until it completely reappeared around five hours later. Elizabeth's parents had already made it clear that she wouldn't be allowed to stay up and see it, so she had a plan up her sleeve. Apart from the television, there were no other lights on in the room as they wanted to enjoy the glow from the moonlight coming in through the windows.

'It feels like something special is about to happen,' she said.

Tom grunted and continued to read his book.

'Don't you think the world suddenly seems magical, Dad?'

He closed it and turned to look at her. 'Well, you don't need a full moon to think that,' he replied. 'We forget to look up, that's the problem. Everyone is so lost in their own world, staring at screens and social media, they forget we're part of a delicate, interconnected ecosystem that exists in a pressurised atmosphere provided by a planet spinning at a thousand miles an hour.'

She laughed, because she knew the door to getting her way had just been unlocked. 'Mr Isaac told us today that the next supermoon eclipse – like this one – isn't until 2050. That's another thirty years away!'

'I'm aware of that, pumpkin,' Tom said, stroking her hair.

She pressed her face harder against his chest. 'It makes me sad,' she continued.

'What does?'

'Well, the fact that you and Mum will, you know…'

'No, I don't. Your mother and I will what exactly?'

'Well, you two will…' She looked down for effect. 'You'll probably both be in heaven by then, so this is the only chance we have to experience it together.'

He sighed and sat up to look at her and those big brown eyes. He raised an eyebrow theatrically and her mouth twitched as she tried not to smile. 'Mary,' he raised his voice, 'your daughter thinks we should all stay up and watch the eclipse because the next time one comes around, you and I will both be pushing up daisies.'

They heard laughter.

'Charming!' Mary said, coming in from the kitchen. 'When is it all happening again?'

'It doesn't begin until the early hours of Monday – 2.34am, to be precise,' Tom said. 'And the eclipse will last until breakfast time.'

'I think that's too late, darling,' Mary said to Elizabeth. 'None of us will be in any fit state to do anything the next day if we've been up half the night.'

Elizabeth's plan was starting to unravel now that her mother was involved. Tom was no match for Elizabeth. But Mary was harder to manipulate and Elizabeth hadn't planned on her being brought into this particular skirmish.

'My thoughts precisely, Mary,' Tom agreed. 'However,' he continued, turning to Elizabeth and smiling, 'I have changed my mind. Events like these are rare and precious and we owe it to ourselves and the world we live in to participate in them. You know, Mary,' he added, 'it wasn't that long ago I knew a young woman who would stay up all night, given half a chance, and still be the first one in the office.'

Mary smiled and sat down next to him. 'That would have been around the time a certain young lady met a charming professor who bewitched her with a lecture on how Mars moved into the orbit of Venus.'

'Please,' Elizabeth said, pulling a face. 'Stop now. I don't want to hear it. You two are gross.'

They both laughed and kissed each other. Elizabeth rolled her eyes and feigned sticking her fingers down her throat. She had watched this scene too many times and it became more unpalatable with each viewing. However, this time it had been worth it. She would get to stay up and see the moon turn blood-red.

The eclipse was now only days away. Against his better judgement, Tom had shared Montague's theory about the full moon with the police and they hadn't seemed interested, even when he'd mentioned the approaching eclipse. Their dismissiveness annoyed him but he took some consolation in knowing that he was no longer relying on them to keep Elizabeth safe. He would finish work early so he could keep an eye on her.

As he made his way to the station for the final time that week, Tom thought about how she would be meeting up with friends shortly at the bottom of the road to walk up through the churchyard to school. He felt a sudden pang, realising that she could be vulnerable at that time. He calmed himself knowing that each time she had disappeared had been at night. He decided to call Mary anyway to talk it over. She agreed that Elizabeth was fine going to school and reminded him that some of the parents with younger children invariably joined the group of friends as they walked over.

He was soon lost in the daily commute and joined a sea of bodies pressed together, trying to ignore each other. His time at the college was uneventful and passed quickly. That was, until he was finishing his final lecture and Mary called him just after 3pm. They often exchanged texts during the day about domestic affairs and invariably what they would eat that evening, so he was surprised to see her name come up as a call. He stepped out of the hall and walked into the corridor. He knew something was wrong when he heard panicked shouts in the background before she came on the line.

'Tom, someone's taken her.'

He felt short of breath. 'What do you mean? They've only just opened the school gates!' he cried. 'What's happened?'

'When I got here, her class teacher said she was collected by her aunt and cousin. Apparently, they were waiting the moment the school opened.'

'Cousin? She doesn't have a bloody cousin! Have they checked the CCTV and called the police? What the hell were they thinking?'

'The police are on their way now.'

'Oh God…' He stormed down the corridor and looked out of the window of his office. 'What were the school playing at, letting her leave with someone we haven't approved?' he roared, tears filling his eyes.

'They don't have to approve them at her age any more. Tom, they're as distraught as we are—'

'I highly doubt that!' he said, banging the phone down on the table.

One of his colleagues mouthed at him through the glass wall of the office, asking if he was all right. Tom shook his head and turned back to the window, putting the phone back to his ear.

'They said they thought Elizabeth knew them as she ran over excitedly to the boy,' Mary explained, now crying herself. 'The teachers heard her call him Tobias.'

Tom slammed his palm against the window and gripped the phone so hard in his other hand, his knuckles turned white. 'I'll be there as quickly as I can,' he promised, his voice sounding dead. 'Give DC Roberts a call and make sure she knows about this.'

He threw open his office door and ran for the stairs, taking them two at a time. When he reached the ground floor, he left the building and sprinted for the station. On the train, he spoke to Mary again and asked her to call Pankhurst and see if he would meet them at the house. He then called Father Montague to ask him to do the same. At the stop before his, a group of schoolchildren got on the train and, for an instant, he thought he saw Elizabeth. He groaned when he realised his mistake, alarming those sitting nearby. He stood up and walked through the carriages to the front, in order to be closest to the exit at the station.

When he got home, Pankhurst and Montague were waiting. The teacher was the only member of staff allowed to leave the school after getting Mary's call. The rest had been called into an emergency meeting to review what had happened. Montague had his arm around Mary, who slipped free and went to Tom. He was breathless and sweating from having run from the station. Pankhurst fetched him a glass of water.

'Thank you, Simon. Thank you both for coming. I don't suppose we've heard anything yet from the police?'

Mary held him tightly. 'No. DC Roberts said she would visit with news the moment they had something.'

Tom told the two men that he needed their help searching for Elizabeth, because they knew her and he trusted them.

'Tell us what you need,' said Father Montague.

Tom asked the priest to come with him and visit Cornelius Draper. He suggested Pankhurst visit the homes of Elizabeth's classmates she was most friendly with to see if any of them knew about Tobias, starting with Freddie Evans.

'Isn't that what the police are going to be doing, Tom?' Pankhurst asked.

'Even if they do, it won't be as quickly as you can do it. And you have the added advantage: the children trust you.'

The teacher nodded and got up to leave. Tom and Montague walked out with him.

'Mary, I've got my phone.'

'I'll call you the minute I hear anything,' she promised. 'You don't think she might come home on her own?'

'I think we've been lucky before,' Tom said. 'This time, they've shown their faces in public and taken her.'

She nodded, not wanting to hear any more. As he closed the door behind them, they heard Mary call out.

'Bring our baby home, Tom.'

Elizabeth hadn't seen Tobias for several weeks. She was also too frightened to go back again on her own to look for the locket, which made it all the more surprising to find him waiting for her after school. She was the first one to be called forward to leave the class. When she heard that her cousin and aunt were waiting for her, Tobias winked before she could say anything to the teacher.

'Tobias! What are you doing here?'

She wanted to introduce him to the other children. The duchess said they had to get back, as she was getting things ready for a special party to celebrate the lunar eclipse and needed to be at the house to continue the preparations. Elizabeth then remembered that Mary was meant to be picking her up from school today.

'We decided it was about time we met your parents.' The duchess smiled. 'Mary was so lovely, and of course was happy for you to come back to ours and play with Tobias this afternoon. We told her we would bring you home before it got too late.'

Elizabeth was shocked to hear this but assumed her mother had agreed to it, otherwise she would have been at the school herself.

It was a short walk to the river where the ferryman was waiting for them. He helped the duchess into the boat, but didn't speak. By the time they had crossed and were heading into the woods, Elizabeth could just make out the edge of the moon, pale in the daylight, slowly emerging on the horizon.

The front gate gave way with a rattle. Tom lifted the gargoyle knocker and let it fall against the front door. After no one answered, he raised his arm and began hammering on the door. The hard timber barely moved and made little noise.

'Is there anyone in there? Mr Draper?' he called.

Father Montague asked if he should try. Tom ignored him and took hold of the door handle and turned it hard to the right. It caught halfway through the turn, so he tried again, using both hands. There was a clunk as the latch on the inside lifted. He pushed the door again; then once more, harder this time, with his shoulder. A puff of dust fell off the top of the frame and coated his head and shoulders. He coughed and spat on the floor.

'No one's been here for years,' he said, turning to the priest.

'Why do you say that?' A smart-looking man in half-moon glasses stood in the hallway. He wore a shirt and bow tie underneath a waistcoat decorated with a gold watch and chain hanging from his breast pocket. The look was ruined by a pair of slippers that had split at the toes, revealing what looked like old cricket socks.

'Mr Draper?' asked the priest.

'That's me. Now, who are you and what are you doing in my house?'

By this time, Elizabeth and Tobias had been playing in the grounds and were now exploring the kitchen garden when Tobias suggested they go inside as it was starting to get dark.

'Are you taking me home now?' she asked.

'Soon. My aunt said we should go upstairs and wait until she's ready.'

He took her to one of the bedrooms, where she went over to the window. She told him she could see the maze. When he didn't reply, she saw he had left the room.

'Tobias?' She walked over to the door. It was locked. She

shook the handle and banged on the door with the palm of her hand. 'Tobias! Let me out – this isn't funny.'

She went over to the window again. No one was out there. Despite her being able to turn the handle, the window remained tightly shut.

Tom and Montague exchanged glances. They were unsure who should speak or what they should say.

'We're so sorry, you must forgive us,' the priest began. 'We weren't sure if anyone still lived here. We were told you might be able to help us—'

Tom stepped between them before Montague could finish. 'My name is Tom Fairchild. My daughter is missing and some lunatic monk seems to think you might know where she is.'

Cornelius Draper closed his eyes and smiled. 'Please come in and tell me more,' he said. 'You mentioned a monk. Do you know his name?'

'Well, how many monks do you know?' Tom snapped. When Draper didn't answer, he put his hands up to apologise and started again. 'I've no idea what his name is,' he said. 'We followed him through the woods out the back there once before,' he added, pointing in the direction they'd come from, 'trying to find a house where he said my daughter had been taken.'

'This is quite terrible,' Draper replied, frowning and pursing his lips. His hands were clasped behind his back. 'And tonight of all nights.'

'The monk said you could help us find the house,' Tom continued.

'Because he couldn't take you there,' said Draper, 'of

course.' Now he was nodding his head. 'And you want me to give you directions to the house in the woods.'

'What I'd really like, Mr Draper, is for you to come and show us how to find it,' Tom said.

'I'm sorry. That's not possible.'

'Mr Draper, forgive us; we have been quite rude. I am Father Montague from St Anne's Church and Tom here is searching for his young daughter, Elizabeth, who is missing. We desperately need your help.' He told Draper of the evening's events and explained in greater detail how the monk had been unable to lead them to the house.

When he finished, Draper said they had misunderstood him. 'Of course I will help you. However, I can't go up there myself. I am not as strong as I used to be and will only slow you down. I can show you on a map where to find the house in the woods.'

The two men followed him down the hall. It was a fine house with generous dimensions and both the ornate floor tiles and the chandeliers were original, but its bookish owner had let it fall into disrepair. Dust lay thick on the floor and banister, and when Tom ran his finger along the rail in the drawing room, it looked like he had rubbed it in charcoal.

'Please excuse the state of the house,' Draper apologised, without turning to look at them. 'I have little interest in housework.'

Tom pulled a face at Montague to ask how Draper knew what they were thinking, then wiped his finger on the seam of his pocket, allowing the fabric of his jeans to strip his fingerprint of the dust. They walked across a threadbare mosaic rug that lay on dark floorboards before stopping in front of a chest of drawers.

'The one you need is in there,' Draper said, pointing to the top drawer that had not been closed properly.

Tom decided against slipping his hand into the drawer, instead opening it further using the carved mahogany handles. Despite already being ajar, it was stiff and he needed to work it up and down to set it free. Inside was a rolled-up parchment bound with black ribbon. He picked it up and bounced the end on the top of the drawers to rid it of dust, then pulled either end of the ribbon and opened it out. The map was familiar. It showed the woods and the path they had walked along by the river, as well as the exit in the wall that ran alongside the road that had by turns led them to Cornelius Draper.

'Now, where did you get to with the monk?' Draper asked.

They looked at the map and then at each other.

Montague put his finger on the spot. 'We reached this area here,' he said, tapping the outline of a tree marked as 'the great oak'. 'And then we went left up here before losing him.' He squinted to focus better before carrying on. 'Then we found him again about here, at this point by a yew tree.'

Draper nodded. 'And it was then he said he could take you no further and suggested you come and ask me.'

'How do you know that?' asked Tom.

'Our friend, the monk, knows the woods as well as anyone. Unfortunately, he can be – how shall I put it? – a trifle superstitious about certain things. No matter – you were very close when he left you. The great oak is the signpost, if you like. When you reach it, you need to turn right here,' Draper said, pointing to a fork in the path, 'then continue until you reach a small shelter. From there, you bear west through this area until you come to a clearing.

Cross the grass and you will see the house through a large row of hornbeams.'

Tom turned to the priest. 'I hope you got that?'

'Yes, I think so,' Montague replied. 'May we take the map with us, Mr Draper?'

'Be my guest.' Draper smiled and raised his arm to shepherd them out of the room. 'I do hope you find your daughter, Mr Fairchild,' he continued. 'It seems we're all looking for something, aren't we?'

Tom took the map off the chest of drawers and led Montague out of the house and into the night.

After leaving Draper's house, they headed for the lane that led to the woods. When they reached the yew tree where they had last seen the monk, they took out the map. Father Montague held it against the trunk of the tree while Tom used the torch on his phone to see where they were. After a quick discussion, they set off again and came to the great oak Draper had described as the signpost. They followed his instructions and took the right fork in the path, passing the small wooden shelter and moving into the clearing. Walking across the grass, they saw the hornbeams and then finally the house. Tom ran past the statue of Father Thames that Elizabeth had seen with Tobias and banged both fists on the front door. When no one answered, he tried the handle, then went to one of the side windows to look inside.

'It looks derelict, Tom,' Montague shouted.

'It doesn't matter,' Tom replied. 'They could still have brought her here.' He ran alongside the house, stopping to peer in each of the windows.

'Tom, look!'

Tom turned to see Father Montague pointing at the roof. 'What? I can't see anything,' he replied. 'You mean the smoke?' He ran around the building to the room with the chimney and saw the embers glowing in the fireplace. 'So someone *is* here. Help me find something to break this window.'

Montague joined him at the side of the house. 'Wait, did you hear that?' He put his hand on Tom's shoulder and pointed past the house to the sculpted hedgerows that marked out the maze. 'I can hear voices, can you?'

Tom stopped for a moment to listen. He heard nothing. 'Come on,' he said and the pair ran over to the entrance. 'Are you sure you heard something?'

The priest told him it sounded like children playing, so Tom called Elizabeth's name. There was no reply, so they carried on and followed the path into the maze until they had a choice of left or right. Tom swore and called again for Elizabeth. Met with silence, the men split up and went in opposite directions.

'Tom, let's keep calling to each other so we don't get lost,' shouted Montague.

They each negotiated their way through the maze before Tom found his path blocked by a green wall of hedging and called to let the priest know. 'Did you hear me?' he shouted after getting no response.

'Yes, sorry – there's something here I think you should see.'

Each retraced their steps to meet where they'd started and then Father Montague led Tom to the point he had reached. In front of them stood the stone marking the centre of the maze and above it, caught on the top of the hedge, was a gold locket.

'Is it…?'

Montague didn't get to finish his question before Tom ran forward and clambered up the stone, carefully retrieving the necklace from a branch. He looked out across the rest of the maze and screamed again for Elizabeth, his voice breaking with emotion, before jumping back down to the ground. He brought the pendant to his lips and started crying.

Elizabeth had fallen asleep on the bed when a noise outside woke her. It took a moment to remember where she was. She jumped up and ran to the window in time to see two people enter the maze. She didn't call for help as they were probably from the house. When they reappeared, one of them was carrying something in his hand that glistened, shining in the moonlight like a beacon at sea. Her gold chain and locket? Her heart leapt when she recognised the shape of the man holding it. She then saw her father's face.

'Listen, Tom, this means we're close. We don't stop now,' Montague was saying.

Tom looked up at him and nodded, wiping his face on his sleeve, and took a deep breath. Montague suggested they go back to the house and see if there was another way in. Then Tom stopped to bend down.

'What is it?'

'Just getting a little help.' He had put Elizabeth's necklace in his pocket and now held a large stone from the perimeter of the driveway to his chest in both hands.

They headed for the window they had looked through earlier. The sound of the rock exploding through the glass caused the birds roosting in the trees to take flight.

'My goodness! I hope there's no one here, Tom.'

'I hope there is. They'll wish they were never born when I get my hands on them.' Tom lifted himself through the broken window and into the room.

At the top of the house, Elizabeth was shouting for him, louder and louder. She was sure he'd heard her when he hurled the stone through the window. She dashed for the door and pulled on it. It remained locked, so she ran back to the window. Her father and the other man – it looked like Father Montague – were already out of sight and climbing through the broken ground-floor window. She could hear them talking and banging around in the room below.

Montague followed Tom through the opening and went over to inspect the fireplace. 'We must have the wrong room, Tom.' He bent down and touched the cold iron of the grate.

'This was definitely it, I'm sure,' Tom said, looking around the room. He tried the door, which was locked, and he kicked it in frustration.

They climbed back through the broken window and stepped away from the house to look over it again. When Elizabeth saw Tom and the priest outside again, she was confused. She cried out for him and hammered on the windowpane with both hands in desperation.

'The monk was telling the truth, then. At least we've got something concrete to share with the police now,' Montague said.

Tom looked at him, and then down at Elizabeth's locket, which he was holding again. 'I'm not leaving here without her.' He started bellowing her name at the top of his lungs.

'We'll keep looking as we go. It's possible she could be making her way home as she did last time,' Montague suggested.

Upstairs, Elizabeth saw her father look down at her locket in his hands, then yell her name. She heard the fear and desperation in his voice. She climbed up and stood on the stone sill to fill the window with her body, and continued to call for him, tears streaming down her face. At one point, she thought he looked straight at her. It was as if she wasn't there, and his eyes continued to scan the rest of the house and grounds for signs of her. When the two men turned and walked away, she collapsed on the floor.

They continued to call for her as they went back through the woods. Midway across the river, Tom cut the boat's engine and listened for the unanswered echo of his own voice bouncing off the water. He scanned the river for signs of life. Nothing moved apart from an old rowing boat that bumped gently against the bank near where they had entered the water.

SIXTEEN

Suffer the Little Children

The disappearance of Elizabeth Fairchild disturbed Montague profoundly. He was used to the defining trinity of births, marriages and deaths. This was different. Before joining the priesthood, he had occasionally reported on depravity in his role as a journalist. The abduction of a young girl from his community unsettled him on a deeper, more personal level. He told himself that it was due to the savage act occurring in such a gentle setting. Even so, it raised questions for him about the nature of his role in the ministry.

It was Sunday morning and she had been missing for two nights. He woke early and listened to the birds celebrate the dawn of a new day. Closing his eyes, he hoped for more sleep. But there were too many unanswered questions and the first light coming through the curtains told his body it was time to rise. He sighed and pushed himself out of bed, careful not to wake his wife, Catherine. He took his dressing gown off the brass hook on the door and went downstairs. When the kettle had boiled, he carried a large cup of tea through to the study and placed it on a stained cardboard beer coaster on his writing desk. He took out a pencil and a piece of paper from the drawer and thought about the sermon he would deliver later that morning. A fine mist from the tea escaped like a genie from a bottle.

Suffer the little children. Was that too obvious? Would it be insensitive to point so directly to Elizabeth? He put down the pencil and took a mouthful of tea. He thought it would be far worse to ignore what had happened, particularly as he would be speaking to people who needed reassurance as well as an explanation of what was going on.

He noticed a songbird land on the stone birdbath and throw thousands of tiny droplets into the air as it shook its body. The water fell on the plants in the flower bed and rolled down their leaves onto the soil. He began to write.

An hour later, he felt a hand on his shoulder.

'Been up long?'

He smiled. 'Long enough for what I needed.'

Catherine raised an eyebrow.

'Today's sermon. I was unsure what to say about Elizabeth.'

'They will be looking to you for guidance.'

He nodded. 'The Lord has told me what to say through his creatures.'

'In that case, you promised me breakfast this morning,' she reminded him, stroking his hair.

St Anne's had a devoted band of parishioners who attended the Eucharist each Sunday. Father Montague was grateful to them for their support. Despite this, their number was small and he longed for the challenge of addressing a wider audience. He also wished for a few new faces to engage with once the service was over.

After breakfast with Catherine, he dressed and walked

over to the church. It was a bright morning and as he went through the graveyard, he was serenaded by a blackbird. He unlocked the church and was soon joined by Mrs Gapper, who helped set out the service sheets. When the bell-ringers arrived, he walked over to the lectern and laid out the notes for his reading.

Fifteen minutes later, he opened the heavy doors to the church. Instead of the usual handful of familiar faces, there was a queue that stretched through the graveyard and onto the street. When he turned to walk over to the pulpit his face was flushed.

'When I thought about what to say today, I did so imagining I was addressing the entire community,' Montague began. 'I'm glad I did, because it seems you're all here today.'

Polite laughter broke out among those in attendance who filled the ground floor, as well as upstairs in the balconies. The overflow stood shoulder to shoulder with their backs to the stained-glass windows.

Montague asked God's forgiveness for their sins and read from one of the Gospels, before inviting Mrs Cuthbertson, the school head teacher, to give a reading. Then came the sermon.

'For many of us, our first experience of the church is baptism. It is when we are officially admitted to the Christian faith and our names are spoken by a priest, in the presence of the Lord, for the first time: "Welcome. Protect this child and bestow upon it the gift of the Holy Spirit. Wisdom, understanding, counsel, fortitude, knowledge, piety, and fear of the Lord." And the use of water is, of course, highly symbolic. It represents purification and the cleansing of sin. This morning I watched a songbird in my garden start the day with a vigorous wash in the birdbath. It flapped its wings and shook its head, sending an arc of water soaring through the air onto the soil. Like us, it relished the fresh beginning; a new start. And the process of discarding the past and embracing the new served to feed the earth. It occurred to me that all living creatures are connected. And the way we live and behave has consequences for all of those around us.

'We are here today united as a community through a shared concern for one of our own. The pain of her disappearance for the parents of Elizabeth Fairchild has been felt by all of us and raised many questions.' Montague paused while there were nods and murmurs of agreement. 'The American clergyman Henry Ward Beecher said, "*Children are the hands by which we take hold of heaven.*" So, how can a benevolent being allow a child to be taken? Why was she taken? How could someone do such a thing? What if it had been my child? What can I do to help? These are all reasonable questions and ones I will address this morning.'

He looked up before taking a deep breath. 'The Lord created us in his image, but we know that our world is subject to more than divine beneficence. The laws of physics teach us that for every action, there is an equal and opposite reaction. And in our lives, there is a constant battle between good and bad, positive and negative, happy and sad. We don't know why Elizabeth was taken. We do know that it was a wicked act, and we pray that she is returned safe and quickly to her loving family.'

He watched as several of them lowered their heads. 'If it was your child, you would want answers, of course you would,' he continued. 'You would also need the support of those around you. Your neighbours and friends and family, and even those you may not know but who have heard what has happened and care deeply for the welfare of you and your child. That is what a Christian community provides. Care, support, love and hope.' He looked around at the rows of nodding heads. 'So what can you do to help? We must pray for Elizabeth to be found and indeed we shall in a moment. What else can we do? In more practical terms, I want every one of us to help the police. Think hard about anything unusual that may have happened in recent days. Speak to your children. Listen to them. Have they been approached by anyone they don't know? Has anyone asked them about Elizabeth? Did they see her, or anyone else for that matter, behaving out of character or doing something that seemed unusual? We know she was taken by a woman and a boy called Tobias. Someone must know these people or at least have seen them before. While it is some relief that this act was not perpetrated by one of our neighbours, it remains highly unlikely that none of us have seen them before or holds some small clue that can be used to help trace Elizabeth.'

This was the biggest congregation of his life and Father Montague had them in the palm of his hand. He allowed his mind to wander and imagine how it must feel to be a bishop or an archbishop speaking to this many on a regular basis. He looked up from his notes to deliver a final reminder. 'So before we pray, please take another moment to think. Give your subconscious access to your memories and let it search for something unusual; for anyone acting suspiciously in light of what has happened here in our town.'

While he spoke, he made a point of addressing those

up on the balcony to make sure everyone felt included. As he took in the unfamiliar faces, scanning from right to left, he looked back at the doorway. A figure moved away over the threshold and headed down the stone steps, causing Montague to momentarily lose track of where he was. Regaining his composure, he invited the congregation to pray. Montague said the Eucharistic Prayer, before reciting the Lord's Prayer. One by one, the people were invited to approach the chancel to receive the body and blood of Christ. Montague was still basking in the success of his sermon when he was snapped out of it by an open mouth in front of him. Panicked, he looked around to see if anyone else had noticed. They had, and the figure's cloak and hood were making them smile. Not sure what to do, Montague put the bread on the man's tongue and made the sign of the cross on his forehead. The monk said nothing and took the wine from the virger.

When the service was over, Father Montague stood outside the church, offering further words of reassurance as people were leaving. At the back of his mind, he realised that it must have been the monk he'd spotted leaving the balcony during the sermon so that he would be one of the first to receive the Eucharist. When everyone had gone, Montague went back inside and sat down to digest what had happened. He was shocked by the unexpected visitor, but was relieved that his sermon had been so well received. And he was happy that he had fulfilled his role as parish priest and provided succour for his flock.

'What about you, Father?'

'I'm sorry?' Montague asked, smiling, and turning to see who it was.

'Have you asked yourself the question you asked of others today?'

Montague knew then who it was. 'You told me you weren't allowed in here,' he reminded the monk.

'That changed when they took the girl.'

Montague looked around to see if there was anyone who could help him.

'I am here to guide you, Father, not harm you.'

'Is everything all right, Father?' It was Mrs Gapper.

Montague looked back at the monk, who was now walking towards the side door. 'Wait!' He ran after him, signalling for Mrs Gapper to wait there. 'What did you mean about asking myself the same question I asked of others?'

The monk stopped. 'Haven't you seen something out of the ordinary that might hold a clue to…' he paused, 'Elizabeth's disappearance?'

Montague realised that the monk now knew Elizabeth's name from today's sermon. 'Me? I haven't seen anything!' he protested.

'This is the second time we've met and I remain a stranger to you. And yet I warned you the girl was in danger.'

Montague put his arm out to the side to steady himself against the wall. 'I did tell people about our encounter,' he stammered, 'but it was obvious you hadn't taken Elizabeth as you were looking for her yourself.'

'Father, no one here knows anything. I am the only one who can help you and there is not much time.'

'Why should I believe you? I don't even know who you are. You're not a monk, that's for sure: there's no monastery around here.'

'You seem certain of what I am not. It is a pity you find it easier to disbelieve than to have faith.'

The words pricked Montague and his face flushed. 'Don't you dare question my belief here,' he hissed.

'You have seen his hand at work – can you not see it here?'

'What do you mean?' Montague whispered.

'A miracle brought you to the church many years ago, did it not, Father? So I ask you this. Having eyes, do you not see?'

Montague swallowed and allowed himself time to think. The monk could not know what had led to his life as a priest. And where was the evidence of a higher power at work in Elizabeth's disappearance? Montague saw only evil, and the man in front of him – the same man who had been too afraid before to enter his church – was somehow involved in her abduction. 'All I see is someone who will not tell me who he is, his name, nor why he wants to find a young girl abducted from this parish,' he replied flatly.

'My name makes no difference, but I will tell you. It is Edmund and I am a monk. I placed my life in servitude since I was a boy; much younger than you did, Father. And I did not need Lazarus to show me the light.'

The reference to the car accident shocked Montague and he sat down on the end of the bench. 'How can you know that?' he asked.

'You wanted a sign and there you have it. I told you there is not much time. If the girl isn't found by the time the great moon reappears, she will be lost forever. You must cross the river and enter the woods when the sun goes down. I will be waiting.' The monk walked towards the open door at the far end of the church.

'Why do you care?' the priest called after him.

The monk's eyes caught the light from the pillar candles that flickered in his pupils as he spoke. 'Because *he* does.'

After the monk had left, Montague went around slowly making sure the place was empty. The volunteers who helped with the service had gone and left the collection box in the sacristy. He got changed and took the donations to deposit them in the safe at the vicarage. Before leaving the building, he poked his head through the curtains that separated the back of the nave from the bell tower to check that the ringers had gone, and then locked the church and crossed the churchyard to his home.

He thought about what Edmund the monk had said to him. Was his arrival in the town really a sign from God? Montague felt uncomfortable in the man's company and found it unimaginable that the Lord would choose such a troubled soul as his messenger. Could that in itself be a lesson? *Do not judge or you too will be judged*, he thought, and shook his head. If the monk really had Elizabeth's best interests at heart, that should make them allies. And if he didn't, why would he still be looking for her when she had already been taken? Then there was the question of motive. Montague unlatched the side gate between the churchyard and the vicarage. The monk cared, 'Because *he* does.'

'This is madness,' Montague repeated dismissively.

'What is, darling?' His wife was emptying a small watering can into the birdbath on the lawn.

'Oh, hello, Catherine. I didn't see you there.'

'What's madness? Not your sermon, I hope?' She laughed.

'No, I think that was well received, don't you?' he asked. 'I had an unexpected member of the congregation. That monk I told you about.'

She put down the watering can and walked over to him. 'Not the one who took the Eucharist! Did you speak to him?'

'He waited for me after the service. He said the Lord had sent him to find Elizabeth.'

Catherine gasped. 'Now I see the madness,' she said.

He put his arm around her and went into the house to lock away the collection money.

'Are you going to tell Tom?' she asked.

'Yes, I have to go and see him. There's something else he should know.' He told her about the rest of his conversation with Edmund and how the monk had said to meet him later that night in the woods.

'You're not going, are you?! The man is clearly deranged.'

'Quite possibly. But what if, just maybe, he's telling the truth?'

Before going to Tom's house, Montague went to the computer in his office. There remained one question the monk had not answered. That was the name of his monastery. Montague wasn't aware of any working monastery in the area and a quick internet search confirmed he was right. In fact, the only one he could find within a fifty-mile radius had closed down some two hundred years ago and was actually not far from where he was meeting Brother Edmund that night.

Tom was on the phone when Mary opened the door to Father Montague. It wasn't long before he ended the call and joined them in the kitchen. 'That was the police. They've got nothing,' he said.

'Have they finished their door-to-door inquiries, Tom?' Mary asked.

'They completed their rounds last night. They've spoken to all the school parents as well as everyone living nearby, and of course the usual persons of interest.'

'What does that mean exactly?'

'Just the local idiots they like to pull in when something bad has happened.' Tom looked at Father Montague and nodded.

The priest gave him a tight smile and said he had some news. He told them about what had happened at the church and his instructions to meet the monk later that night in the woods.

'Call the police, Tom. Now!' Mary instructed.

'Hold on a minute, let me think about this.' Tom turned to Montague. 'What do you think? We probably should let the police handle this. We don't know who this character is. He's obviously involved somehow and they should be able to get the truth out of him.'

'Ordinarily, I would agree, of course I would, Tom, but something strange is going on and I'm not sure what the police can do,' Montague said.

'Why do you say that?' Mary asked.

'Because he didn't even say where to meet exactly. Just to cross the river and come to the woods at dusk and he'll find us.'

'That's ridiculous!' Tom exclaimed.

'I know. It must mean he's going to be watching us cross the river, and if the police come instead of us, I can't imagine he'll show himself.'

Tom sighed.

'You're not going, Tom,' Mary said, crossing her arms.

'What choice do I have?'

Unable to argue any more, she started to cry and he did too.

'Dear God, just be careful then, Tom. You too, Father. And please find her,' Mary said, stroking her husband's arm.

SEVENTEEN

Heaven Awaits the True

Elizabeth had been shut in the room in the house for two nights without food or water when she heard someone outside the door. 'Who's there? Tobias, is that you?' she cried.

'I'm sorry.'

'Sorry?! What do you mean, you're sorry? Let me out of here now!' she howled.

'It's not locked.'

She tried the handle and the door opened. In front of her on the floor was a loaf of bread and a bottle of milk. She picked them up and quickly drank some of the milk. 'Why are you doing this to me? I saw my father last night in the garden. He was looking for me. I want to go home.'

'You can't. Not yet.'

'Why not?' She started to sob.

'I wanted you to watch the eclipse of the moon with me.'

'What?! Are you mad? You could've just asked me to do that! You didn't have to kidnap me.' She stared at him as she tore another chunk off the bread and washed it down with the remainder of the milk.

'I was worried you wouldn't be allowed out late to watch it,' he explained.

She shook her head in despair and finished the food. 'Where's everyone else?'

'Getting ready for the party. Elizabeth, do you remember what I told you about Solomon's book predicting the future?'

She shrugged.

'Well, he told me it says that tonight's eclipse is magical and something special is going to happen.'

'So what, Tobias?'

'I want you to read it to me.'

She thought for a moment. 'Only if you take me home afterwards.'

He nodded.

'A penny for your thoughts.' Charles Featherstone had placed his hands on Gabriella's shoulders and looked back at her in the mirror.

She sat at her dressing table and stared at him.

'What is it, my love? What troubles you?' her husband asked.

She closed her eyes. 'Do you think we'll ever be free?'

It was a question that had troubled them for as long as they could remember. Their early days had been a carousel of exotic travel, social engagements, and exciting new acquaintances. Over time, the only parties they'd come to attend were the ones they hosted and the faces stayed the same. Charles loved how Gabriella brought a little devil to their relationship. She was nobody's fool and beneath her attractive exterior lay the heart of a dragon. That was both exciting and challenging, and meant it was rare that anyone got the better of the duke and duchess. This made their current predicament all the more confusing. It was as though a spell had been cast on the house and they were powerless to resist. Only Solomon claimed to have the answer and was convinced his stolen book would help them navigate their way out of the stupor they found themselves in. No one else had any other ideas.

'We were free before and will be again,' Charles reassured her. The librarian has made a convincing case for the provenance of the book and its prophetic value. We should keep faith in him.'

'You didn't think that the other night,' she replied, a smile playing on her lips.

'I find it hard to stomach what we must do, that is all.'

'What *we* must do?'

'What *I* must do,' he corrected himself.

Gabriella stood up and laughed before kissing him. 'Oh no, husband dearest, this time you must allow me,' she said, licking her lips while running a finger under his chin.

By the time they reached the Octagon, Elizabeth was cold. Despite the bread and milk, she was still hungry and her body twitched as she started to shiver.

'What's the matter?'

'What do you mean?' she asked.

'You're shaking.'

She rolled her eyes. 'I'm shivering, Tobias,' she snapped. 'And why don't you feel the cold? You've never got enough clothes on.'

'Well, I obviously have,' he replied, 'because I'm not cold.'

She thought for a moment. 'Well, if you're so clever, why do you call this place with an altar "the Octagon" instead of a chapel?'

'Because it's got eight sides,' he explained.

They stared at each other before laughing. She didn't want to and was still angry with him, but couldn't help herself. She felt like she did at the dinner table when her parents told her to stop sniggering and the more she tried, the harder she laughed. Before long, she tasted a tear on her lip and had to sniff hard to stop her nose running, wiping away the trace with the back of her hand.

'We must be quiet,' Tobias said, his eyes still filled with fun. 'You know how protective Solomon is over the book.'

The bright light that had illuminated the gardens when they'd left the house started to dim as the moon moved into the earth's shadow. They got up from underneath the window and walked up the steps to the entrance to the chapter house, turning the handle in one movement. Leaving the door open, Elizabeth stepped over the threshold and into the building. After taking several steps towards the altar, she heard the door close behind her. Turning quickly, she saw it wasn't Tobias.

'I thought you weren't able to come to the house?'

'This place is nothing to do with that house,' Edmund replied, approaching her. 'Why will you not stay away?' he asked.

Once again, he was between her and her escape route.

'I've done nothing to you,' she said. 'What do you want with me?' Not waiting for an answer, she panicked and shouted, 'Tobias!'

The monk raised a finger to his lips. 'Be quiet, Elizabeth. That boy will not help you. He has led you into a trap.'

The sound of his words had barely decayed when she heard whispered voices and felt a cold draught. 'What's that?' she asked, panic in her voice.

'Now you are here, the boy has summoned them.'

To escape, she had to pass within the monk's reach. If she didn't try, she would be trapped and outnumbered. She dashed for the door. Edmund reached for her. She ducked instinctively, brushing the crown of her head against the underside of his tunic sleeve. She reached the door and twisted the handle with all her strength.

'No, child, wait!' he shouted, but she was past him.

She felt the door swing towards her and jumped down onto the path outside. As she hit the ground, her knees buckled and she stumbled forward. Regaining her balance, she looked up and saw Tobias. She heard the whispering again, louder this time, and noticed a row of faces stretched out across the clearing behind him.

'The book has spoken; the prophecy is upon us!' Solomon cried with his arms raised towards the heavens.

The others began chanting, 'Find the golden girl.' Tobias stepped back and was now joining in with them.

Elizabeth tried to swallow, but her tongue scraped across the roof of her mouth. She found it hard to believe this was really happening. She heard her own thoughts as if someone was speaking them: *Your only chance is to run now, harder than you've ever run before. Get away from them and run for your life!* As she assessed which direction to go, she saw movement at the edge of the woods and realised it was

Edmund calling her. He was now crouching low between two bushes with his arms outstretched.

'Elizabeth, you have to trust me. Delay any longer and you'll never see your family again.'

She tried swallowing once more and the muscles in her throat squeezed tightly against themselves. Taking a deep breath, she dipped her head and pulled her feet free from their imaginary prison and sprinted towards the woods. It was only a few feet to where he was waiting. It felt more like a hundred as she pumped her arms and lifted her knees to clear the ground. The chanting continued and she dared not look behind her. When she was within arm's reach of Edmund, Tobias called out in terror.

'No, Elizabeth! He's evil; you must not go with him. We won't hurt you. We worship you!'

His words slowed her momentarily and broke her concentration. Her right boot caught in a tuft of long grass and she lost her balance, pitching head first towards Edmund. Her face was now inches away from him, but she was no longer certain that he offered safety. She pushed herself up and spat mud off her lips. She turned to look for Tobias, who had stayed in line with the others, fists clenched by his sides like a toddler throwing a tantrum.

'I have done nothing to earn your distrust,' Edmund urged. 'They took you and kept you from your family, and used the boy to lure you here.'

She was overwhelmed with homesickness thinking about her parents.

'Child, you know this is a trap. There is no time left.'

'Why did Tobias want me to read the book?' she demanded.

'Because he wanted you in the chapter house.'

'Why?'

When Edmund didn't answer, she made up her mind. If all of this was because of that book, then she had to find it and see what it had to do with her. She jumped up, sprinting back in the direction she had come from. By the time she reached the door, they were nearly upon her. Struggling to catch her breath, she yanked hard on the handle and threw herself inside. She saw that the key was in the door and turned it in the lock. Crossing the short distance to the altar, she stood on tiptoes and started to read where the book had been left open. Her eyes scanned across the lines as she tried to make sense of them.

The earth is full of wonder,
But heaven awaits the true.
To cross the great divide,
A child must believe in you.
When the river breaks its banks
And the blood moon fills the sky,
You must find the golden girl
And follow her on the tide.

'Why on earth do they think I am the golden girl?!' she shrieked.

There was movement to her left and she spun round. Like a priest at communion clasping both hands in front of his chest, there was Solomon.

'You have already answered that question,' he said, smiling triumphantly. 'The passage you just read is a prophecy. You have come here now at this time of heavenly eclipse to save us and have shown that you are indeed the golden girl.'

She turned to see the others enter the building. The key was no longer in the door. They were repeating their incantation. As Elizabeth looked at Solomon, he was doing the same. She knew there was no escape. They were standing between her and the door. She wished she had taken her chances in the wood with Edmund. Now she was outnumbered and trapped inside.

She was thinking of what she could say to try and talk her way out when a man's voice shouted for silence. The group parted and Charles Featherstone stepped forward. He looked at her, then up at the window and the moonlight that illuminated the dust particles, casting its soft spotlight on her face.

'You truly are a golden girl,' he said and bowed his head. 'Your presence humbles us.'

'What do you want with me?' she pleaded. 'I've done nothing to any of you. I just want to go home.'

'We all want to go home,' replied Solomon, to which the others cheered.

Charles raised his hand to silence them. He looked at Gabriella, who now stood beside him.

'Here we are as if walking down the aisle again together, dearest,' she said.

Elizabeth saw Tobias and looked into his blue eyes, silently pleading for help. He looked away. 'Tobias?' she said, her voice breaking.

A flash of light caught her eye and she saw a blade in Gabriella's hand.

'What are you doing?' she whimpered. Tiny dots of light filled her vision as she tried to catch her breath.

Solomon and the two men who had chased her before with Tobias were now standing either side of her.

'Elizabeth?'

She flinched when she realised someone was calling her from outside.

'*Elizabeth!*

'Dad! Dad! I'm in here – help me, please!' she screamed.

The shouting created a distraction and she bolted for the door past the duke and duchess. Outside, she shouted again for her father but couldn't see him. She knew she had to keep running and headed for the spot in the woods where she had seen the monk. She navigated a path through the bushes and long grass, feeling the twigs brush and flick against her arms as she ran. Her legs were getting tired and she was finding it harder to clear the overgrowth that tugged at her feet. There was still no sign of him. She called again, while maintaining a course along the makeshift path. At the point of collapse, she heard her name being shouted. She bent over with her hands on her knees, breathing hard, and checked they weren't following her.

'Don't worry; you have left them behind.'

She looked up to see Edmund. 'Where did you come from?'

'I was waiting for you.'

'Where's my father?'

'I don't know. You must come with me now or they will take you.'

She remembered her mistake of not going with him before. 'Where are we going?'

'Across the river. They have waited a long time for this moment and won't want to let it pass again.' He led her further along the track through the woods.

'Please tell me what is going on,' she pleaded, sobbing again.

'There is no time. I have to get you to the ferryman before it's too late.'

As she followed, she replayed the events of the evening in her mind. Her disbelief at Tobias betraying her and the horror of seeing the knife in the duchess's hand. 'Tobias said they worship me,' she called out. 'So why did they try and kill me?'

'You must keep walking. We don't have long.'

She ran a few steps to catch up with him.

'The book the librarian possesses is very old and holds great power over those who read it,' Edmund explained. 'The people from the house stole it from my monastery many years ago because they think it tells of the future.'

'Is that what you believe?' Elizabeth asked.

'I'm trying to find out.'

The path, which had been lit so brightly by the moon, was now less clear. They both noticed and looked up at the sky. The perfect white circle was tarnished by a shadow.

'The lunar eclipse.'

'You know about that?' he asked.

'Of course; everyone does,' she said.

He looked back to make sure they weren't being followed. 'They want you because the book talks of a blood moon and the coming of a golden girl.'

'But what makes them think that's me? That's crazy!'

'They have waited many years for this moment and are certain of it.'

'If I'm so special, why would they harm me? Tobias even said they worship me.'

'They believe you are a gift from God sent to save them.'

She shook her head and clenched her fists in frustration. 'None of this makes any sense at all,' she shouted. 'How can I save them? I don't even know what they want saving from.'

There was a noise behind them and movement among the trees less than two hundred yards away. The monk picked up the pace. Elizabeth started running again to keep up.

'Wait, please! If they capture me again, there must be something I can do,' she pleaded.

'Child, I told you before: they are lost. They think you can help them find their way.'

'How can I do that?'

'That is very simple,' he replied. 'You must die.'

EIGHTEEN

Silent Prayer

Edmund left her at the edge of the trees. Clearing the woods, she made for the river. It was grey and impassive and flowed towards her, pushing her back towards her pursuers. When she reached the bank, she headed for where the boat was moored. She caught sight of them getting closer and was shocked at the fury on their faces. Turning away, her mind captured a snapshot of wide eyes and flaring nostrils and shrieking mouths. The image caused her to lose concentration and miss a clump of long grass at the side of the path. It tugged the toe of her boot and she tripped, pitching headlong towards the river. Her face hit the ground, knocking her teeth together. She felt a burning sensation on her right cheekbone. Lifting her head, she saw a pair of boots inches from her face. They couldn't have caught her that quickly, she thought, suddenly relieved at the thought of being rescued. Pushing herself up on her hands and knees, the smile died on her lips as she looked into the eyes of the ferryman.

'Going somewhere, miss?' he laughed, placing his hands on his knees as he bent down in front of her.

She screamed and then froze at what she saw over his shoulder. Confused, he turned to look. Coming into focus on the river, out of the low mist that clung to the surface, was the large boat that had nearly capsized his ferry. It had a weathered bow and a thick mast that reached for the stars. A herald of white water rippled ahead of the bow as it swept downstream. There was no wind and no sail. A dozen oars on each side propelled it, making a rhythmic sloshing sound as they cut through the water. When it was nearly level with them, the oars remained in the water to slow its progress, allowing the vessel to come to a gradual stop. Without taking his eyes off it, the ferryman reached out to grab Elizabeth's arm. She pushed off hard with both feet in the opposite direction. Her right foot slipped on the muddy bank and she fell again, this time into the river.

She went under immediately and swallowed, causing her to gag and inhale the filthy, cold water. Through the surface, she could make out the shadow of the boat above her and saw the people from the house standing next to the ferryman on the bank. Expecting one of them to reach in and grab her, she saw that their appearances had changed. They were now calm as they looked across at the boat and pointed to where she was. The last person she saw was Tobias smiling at his aunt.

Darkness. Elizabeth knew she was dying. Her body was weightless as she drifted with the current. Still shocked by the boy's betrayal, she was devastated at leaving her parents. They would never know what had happened. Would they ever find her body? As her head turned in the water, she saw the blurred outline of a face moving towards her and an outstretched arm. It was Maurice, the school caretaker. What was he still doing in the river?

A flash of light was followed by a sharp pain in the side of her head, then a stabbing sensation in her abdomen. Instinctively, she reached for her midriff. A second later, she broke the surface, clinging to the end of a thick wooden staff. She was fifty yards downstream on the opposite bank from where she had entered the water. When her body hit the ground, the contents of her lungs and stomach came out of her nose and mouth. Clearing the water enabled her to breathe again. Her choking subsided. Behind her, mist recaptured the part of the river she had disturbed as it continued its journey to the sea without her. She lay on her side on a muddy bank where people stood to go fishing. Her legs remained in the water. She was so cold, she found it impossible to breathe other than in panicked, irregular gasps that shook her body.

'Try and breathe more slowly, child.'

She looked up to see Edmund holding on to the other end of the stick.

'I was foolish for thinking the ferryman would help you. You're safe now.'

She did as she was told and the hyperventilating eased. She heard shouts coming from the woods. Her relief at not having drowned had made her forget that she was being chased. She tried clambering up the bank, then slipped and fell back to where she'd started. She reached again for the wooden staff, but Edmund had gone. Panicking, she whirled her arms in a frantic crawl, trying to pull herself up the bank and out of the river. She was weak and her wet body offered no purchase on the soft ground.

She heard voices across the water and knew it wouldn't be long before they saw her. Out of the corner of her eye, she caught sight of a flash on the water. Focusing on where it had come from, she saw it again; slower this time. The clouds parted overhead and the reflection of the moon emerging from eclipse was imprinted on the rippling surface. Exhausted, she turned onto her back. She remembered how her parents had told her that she was born under a full moon and had always been fascinated by it. Even now, she took comfort in seeing it shine down. She wondered if it would save her. Her father had told her that its gravity moves our oceans, lakes and rivers and is thought by some to affect people's sleep and moods. She thought about his promise to always protect her and felt a heavy tear rest on her cheek, reluctant to continue its descent and leave the memories behind. She refused to give up without trying to reach him and started calling for him with all her might.

Tom was exhausted. The monk had not met them in the woods and there was no sign of life at the house. It had grown colder as the mist had come down and his clothes were damp. It was also getting darker as the eclipse was now well under way.

'Tom?'

There were tears in Tom's eyes when he turned round.

'I thought I heard something,' Montague said.

'Where?'

'Are you OK?' the priest asked, reaching out for him.

'Where?!' Tom shouted, causing Montague to stop in his tracks.

'Listen.'

They stood motionless.

'I can't hear…'

'Why don't you try calling her again?' Montague urged.

Tom did as he was told and his voice reverberated around the woods, accompanied by the rustling of the leaves.

'There! Did you hear it?' the priest asked.

Still shaking his head, Tom's eyes widened when he did hear the faintest echo trying to reach him through the web of branches. 'Elizabeth! Elizabeth!' he shouted, taking off at full tilt in the direction of her cries.

He had not exercised properly for a long time and yet was still able to cross the ground with surprising speed. He picked his knees up high to clear any undergrowth that might trip him. Lungfuls of oxygen had replaced the emptiness in his chest as he held his breath to sprint faster. He knew Montague wouldn't be able to keep up. Something told him that if he was to find Elizabeth, he had to be quick. Feeling dizzy, he exhaled hard. He then took several deep breaths before shouting her name again to check his bearings. This time, her cries were closer and coming from the left of the ancient yew tree. As he burst past it, stiff branches punched and flicked at his body and sharp needles scratched his face. He used his forearm to push them away, while his thighs burst through a rugby tackle of boughs that tried to grab his legs. When he was clear, he found himself on high ground, looking down onto the footpath and the river. He stood at the edge on a crumbling brick wall and brought his hands up to his mouth to project his voice, while turning his head to look for movement. He saw something behind him and was surprised to see Montague wrestling with the yew tree. He went back and pulled him clear.

'Thank you, Tom,' Montague panted. 'Any sign?'

Tom shook his head and called again for her. Montague joined him and their voices rang out, carrying far across the river and into the fields beyond.

'Daddy! Daddy, I'm over here!'

The men followed her cries to the river. They couldn't see her. Then they realised why. She must be in the water by the far bank. Tom jumped down first, hitting the path below and rolling to break his fall. Father Montague landed moments later, tumbling onto his backside with a groan before falling into their boat. Tom untied the craft from the bank and pulled the starter cord, throwing the pair swiftly into the middle of the river before crossing to the other side. Reaching the bank, he drew breath to call for her when he recognised a child's red school coat at the side of the water. He screamed her name when he realised she was still wearing it. Her body was partly submerged in the river, with just her head and shoulders resting on the shore. She raised an arm before losing consciousness and slipping back into the water.

When they got there, Tom clambered up the bank and ran over to where she was before sliding feet first into the river. He was shocked at how cold it was, cutting through his trousers and cramping his legs. 'Come quickly, Father,' he shouted.

The priest appeared on the bank and scrambled down to help. Together, they put Elizabeth's arms across their shoulders and hauled her up onto the path.

'She's cold, Tom,' Montague said, removing his coat and laying it over her.

Tom checked her airways before cradling her head in

his hands and bringing his face close to hers. 'Elizabeth, it's Daddy. Can you hear me?'

When she didn't respond, he looked at Montague, who asked if she was breathing.

'I think so; I'm not sure,' Tom replied.

Montague bent down and put his cheek close to the girl's nose and mouth. 'I don't think she is,' he said, pinching her nose and putting his mouth over hers. As his breath passed into her, he remembered how powerless he had felt attempting this with Marcel Clyde. The boy's mother had said that Montague had breathed life into him, which Montague knew wasn't true. But someone had breathed life into her son and Montague needed his divine help again. As he watched the girl's chest rise and fall with his efforts, he gave a silent prayer. After several attempts, he began chest compressions. On the second press, Elizabeth's body convulsed and water was forced from her lungs and down her cheek. He gave her mouth-to-mouth again, and this time her chest started to lift and fall on its own. 'Thank God,' he said, standing up and making way for Tom, who knelt down and wiped the water away from her mouth. He called her name. Still no response.

'Slap her, Tom. If she's unconscious, she's at risk of hypothermia.'

Tom hit her gently, twice.

She started murmuring and moved her head. 'Daddy…' She looked at him and started to cry.

He picked her up and squeezed her cold, limp body against his. When he looked at Montague, they all had tears in their eyes. Tom reached for him and all three embraced and cried, their tears like the ripples on the water that drifted effortlessly by, catching the light of a golden moon that had cast off its shadow.

Mary saw them as they approached the gate. She threw open the back door and ran out into the garden, barefoot across the grass.

'She's fine, Mary. We've got her. Everything's OK,' Tom said, still carrying Elizabeth in his arms.

Mary reached for her, brushing wet hair from the girl's face. She gasped when she saw a nasty red welt where Elizabeth had banged her cheek falling into the river. 'My baby, what happened to you?'

Tom turned to Montague. 'Please help take her in,' he said, passing Elizabeth to the priest before hugging and kissing his wife. 'She's safe now, Mary. Let's all get inside.' He told her that they had nearly given up hope of finding Elizabeth in the woods until Father Montague heard her cries for help. When he said they'd found her in the river, Mary fell to her knees and started crying.

Montague put Elizabeth down on the sofa and crouched next to Mary. He put his arms on her shoulders and told her to slow down and breathe. Elizabeth was safe now, he told her, and she must stay calm for her sake. The priest telephoned for an ambulance before calling DC Roberts.

They then helped Elizabeth upstairs and ran her a hot bath. Her lips had a blue rim and her teeth chattered when Mary came in to help her get undressed.

When Elizabeth arrived at the hospital, she was wrapped in a silver blanket. The hospital lights reflected off the foil and radiated around her body. She had a private room, where a nurse gave her oxygen and inserted a saline drip. The mask on her face made her panic and she grabbed Mary's arm.

'It's just oxygen to help you breathe more easily,' the nurse said, adjusting the elastic strap around the back of Elizabeth's head, before leaving the room.

There was a knock at the door and two police officers entered. Roberts was one of them. After speaking to Tom and Mary, they introduced themselves to Elizabeth and pulled up chairs next to her bed. They told her that she was safe and they would protect her. The doctors and nurses would help her get her strength back and then she could go home with her mother and father. But it was important that they find the people who had attacked her, they explained. Until the questions started, Elizabeth watched them with wide eyes, saying nothing. When they told her they needed her help, she closed them until tears seeped out of the corners and ran down her cheeks.

'Darling, you won't ever see them again. The police must catch these people so they can't hurt anyone else,' Mary said.

Elizabeth kept her eyes shut and said nothing. Mary thought back to when Elizabeth had misbehaved as a child and would close her eyes to avoid confrontation.

Tom squeezed Mary's hand and reached over to wipe a tear from Elizabeth's face. 'Sweetheart, you don't need to open your eyes or speak louder than a whisper. Please tell us where you were.'

He saw goosebumps on her upper arm and her breathing got heavier. The screen above her bed emitted a series of loud beeps and they saw her heart rate pass 160 beats per minute. There were footsteps in the corridor and the door flew back. The nurse came in, followed by a doctor. The doctor brushed the nearest police officer aside and checked the electrodes on her chest, before increasing Elizabeth's fluids. She then told Elizabeth to look at her. She reached over and used a thumb and forefinger to lift one of Elizabeth's eyelids. The eye looked up into the top of her head as if she were asleep. The alarm on the heart monitor continued to sound and now read 190.

'OK, I'm giving more sedative.' The doctor took a syringe and raised it to check the level.

Tom stood up and started shouting, asking what was happening. One of the police officers held him by the shoulders and moved him away from the bed.

'It's probably a panic attack. Her heart rate is too high and we need to bring it down,' the doctor said. As she took the needle from Elizabeth's arm, the alarm stopped and the monitor showed her heart rate slowing.

Mary stroked her daughter's face and reassured her while the nurse readjusted the oxygen mask again before turning to the police officers.

'Right, I need both of you to go now, please.'

The policeman looked at his boss, who nodded. Before leaving, DC Roberts told Tom they would be in touch later. After they had gone, Tom sat in the chair next to Elizabeth's bed and put his head in his hands.

'Mr and Mrs Fairchild, it's really important that Elizabeth is allowed to rest now without further disturbances,' the doctor said. 'Her body is still in shock and needs time to recover.'

Tom nodded and sighed. He looked at his daughter in the hospital bed and was struck by how pale and vulnerable she looked. Mary's face was tight with worry and he could see that she was close to tears again. He stood up, pushed his chair back, and walked out of the room. Mary called after him. He was already halfway down the corridor as the door closed itself.

Tom found Father Montague by the coffee machine and told him what had happened. Then he asked if he would go with him back to the river.

'Whatever for, Tom?'

'It was only by the grace of God, as you would have it, that we found her. I'm not prepared to wait for next time.'

'What do you mean?'

'They will still be looking for her. It's the best chance we have of catching them and putting a stop to this once and for all.'

'And how will you do that?'

They turned to see Mary marching towards them.

'You listen to me, Tom Fairchild. This nightmare has to stop now!' she said, stamping her foot.

'I'm only trying to protect her, Mary.'

'And you do that by staying here with her and then taking us both home. You let the police do their job finding that boy and his family.'

'Well, they've been pretty useless at that so far, haven't they?'

Before Mary could reply, Montague intervened. 'May I make a suggestion?'

They both looked at him.

'I think you are both right. And there is a good chance that we will come across these lunatics if we go back out there now,' he said, raising his hands to placate Mary. 'However, I also agree with Mary that your place is here with your family, Tom.'

'Well, that's brilliant. So how exactly can I do both?' Tom snapped.

'I'll go,' Montague replied.

'You can't do that. It's not safe for you either,' Mary warned.

Tom nodded. 'Mary's right,' he said. 'It needs at least two of us, but I appreciate the offer.'

Then Mary had an idea. She told Tom to call the police and see if they would send a patrol car to meet Montague at the church, explaining that he could show them where he and Tom had been looking when they'd found Elizabeth.

'Thank you, Father,' Tom said, shaking his hand and wishing him luck.

Mary hugged Montague goodbye before taking her husband's arm and walking back down the neon-lit corridor towards Elizabeth's room. For the first time, she noticed the nasty red welts on his face and reached up to touch them. He took her hand and explained he had got into an argument with a yew tree just before he found Elizabeth.

When Montague got back to the vicarage, a police car was waiting outside the church. Two young officers got out and introduced themselves before the three of them drove out of the town and across the river. After parking the vehicle, they set off for the towpath. Before long, they had left the sound of traffic and the street lights behind. Despite the eclipse having passed, it was overcast now and there was little light to guide them. One of the officers unhooked a torch from his belt and illuminated the path in front of them.

Montague showed them the route he had taken with Tom and explained again what had happened after the monk had visited them. When they reached Nightshade Wood, the gloom made it harder to navigate, despite both officers now using their torches. The priest became unsure which of the trees he had passed earlier, and the paths through the woods seemed more overgrown and difficult to navigate than he could remember.

Finding themselves lost, the policewoman suggested they leave the woods and head for the river to the spot where Montague and Tom had found Elizabeth. When they got there, the current was running quickly and the other officer remarked that it was a miracle they had managed to pull her out alive. Montague thought for a moment back to the car crash and Marcel Clyde, and wondered if they were comparable.

'So you found her over there against the far bank?' one of the officers asked.

'Yes; she was barely conscious and I think she must have floated downstream,' Montague said, pointing to their right.

'And you think she had come from this side of the river?'

'I believe so. She said she had come from the house through the woods. I don't know, of course, if she came straight across or drifted along the edge before we found her.'

They looked across to the other side. It was virtually impossible to make out anything beyond the odd bush, despite the officers directing their torchlight across the water. They told Montague they would take him back over the river so that he could show them exactly where they'd found Elizabeth. When they got there, it was still difficult to see much and the policewoman said it would be better to wait until morning.

'I'm sure you're right,' Montague sighed, looking around in the hope of making out a figure or something suspicious on the towpath. 'We thought we might spot them still looking for Elizabeth.'

'It's too dark now to find anything. And, as we can't see

any other torches, I think it's safe to say no one is looking for her now.'

When they reached the first of the houses on the edge of town, a small wooden boat ran downstream past them, its oars tucked into the hull to avoid any resistance. Its presence surprised the waterbirds settling down for the night and Montague turned to look.

'What's that over there?' he shouted, pointing towards the river.

The officers looked. They couldn't see anything. 'Where?'

'Just past the first house,' Montague said. 'I thought I saw a boat.'

They ran back alongside the house in the direction they'd come from, knowing that anything on the water would drift past. Their torches lit the stretch immediately in front of them and reflected off the vapour that kissed the surface of the water.

'There!'

They shone their torches towards the side of the house. There was movement and the torchlight picked out a pair of red eyes that came at them across the water. The priest cried out as he fell. The police officers crouched next to him with their arms above their heads for protection as the bird soared over them and took off for the trees.

'I think I've had more than enough excitement for one night,' Montague said, trying to laugh as the other two picked him up.

The adrenaline wore off as they walked and the police officers discussed how to describe being attacked by a barn owl in their report. When they reached the bend in the road, the ferryman put the oars back in the boat and emerged from behind the house. The current took him silently downstream towards the woods.

*

Elizabeth was now home from hospital. Her window was open and her bedroom smelt fresh from the night air. Dawn touched the glass and created dancing silhouettes on the curtains.

Tom breathed deeply as he looked at her and thought that this moment was the closest he would get to heaven. Her duvet rose and fell with the rhythm of her life. A lock of golden hair fell across her pale skin. On the bedside table was the locket Mary's mother, Xena Pallas, had given to Elizabeth when she was a little girl. The first light from the crack in the curtains played on its golden links and the monogrammed pendant featuring Xena's initials.

Since Elizabeth had gone missing, Tom had found it difficult to sleep and he was now attuned to waking through the night. He closed his eyes and thought of when he'd first seen her in Mary's arms in the hospital. The intervening years had been the happiest of his life and given him purpose, as well as a new companion with whom he felt the deepest bond. The thought of losing Elizabeth was too much and he squeezed his eyes tight to stop the tears.

A hand touched his.

'I knew I'd find you here. She's safe, Tom,' Mary said.

He tipped his head to rest on hers. Elizabeth's breathing became shallow and they knew she would wake soon.

Acknowledgements

You would not be reading this if it weren't for the belief and commitment of my agent Jenny Todd. A first book is an exercise in self-doubt, so I am also indebted to the endless encouragement of early readers Rosie Nixon, Geordie Greig and Alan Edwards, as well as Stephen Fry, who provided the title.

Thank you to Kealey, Emma and Fiona at FMCM, the finest publicists in the business. Also my gratitude to my copy editor, Faye Booth. The cover design is the work of Paul Denton, and I am grateful for the advice of Chris Duggan.

Finally, I would like to thank my family for their love and support and belief in everything I do